T0351426

NO STORM, JUST WEATHER

THE GERMAN LIST

JUDITH KUCKART

# NO STORM, JUST WEATHER

TRANSLATED BY ALEXANDER BOOTH

LONDON NEW YORK CALCUTTA

This publication has been supported by a grant from
the Goethe-Institut India

**Seagull Books, 2023**

Originally published in German as *Kein Sturm, nur Wetter*
by Judith Kuckart
© DuMont Buchverlag, Cologne, 2019

First published in English translation by Seagull Books, 2023
English translation © Alexander Booth, 2023

ISBN   978 1 8030 9 148 8

**British Library Cataloguing-in-Publication Data**
A catalogue record for this book is available from the British Library

Typeset by Seagull Books, Calcutta, India
Printed and bound by Hyam Enterprises, Calcutta, India

# CONTENTS

**1**

No Storm, Just Weather

**205**

*Acknowledgements*

**206**

*Translator's Notes*

**23.12**

Last night a young woman came up to my bed and put down a bottle of Borjomi next to me, the mineral water Brezhnev used to drink against his vodka hangovers. The woman in my dream would like to say something, I can see that. She tugs the blanket straight, folds a sweater, gathers up my stockings. At last she says, So much snow and so much light in the darkness.

She's wearing a thin grey coat.

SUNDAY

Where are you flying?

I'm not flying anywhere, you?

Siberia, he says, May I sit down?

Si-be-ri-a, she repeats to herself and thinks, My God, is he young.

Last autumn she got into the habit of going out to Tegel Airport, preferably at the weekends. Those are the easier days. When she's lucky her table, the one she refers to as hers, in the cafe in the departures hall is unclaimed. The moment the evening's first flights show up on the display she orders a small beer. Today too she will sit here until the last bus back to town. There's a kind of uneventfulness to it, not unlike meditation. On this early Sunday evening a long dog walks past, a dog like a sausage with a head, pulling a small man behind it. Yesterday, on her way home, a woman with lace gloves sat behind the bus driver and spoke softly in his direction. Stepping off the bus she wondered, Will the woman go home with him once his shift is over and take off her gloves?

Tegel Airport, main hall. On the arrival and departure boards the city names, flight numbers, times and gates ceaselessly change.

In the past, the movement was accompanied by a clacking sound. Now it is digitized and silent.

The flight to Zurich has left its place at the top and is now on its way into the skies over Berlin.

Can I order you something else to drink?

She looks into the blue eyes of the man who is about to fly to Siberia. They are the same blue as the checks of his flannel shirt. With his large hands he can no doubt lay electrical cable and coax the apple trees along the sunny garden wall into growing along a trellis. He probably drives an old estate car with enough room for his wife, two or three kids and a big dog, as well as crates of beer from the beverage shop. Whenever he's not travelling, that is. He's probably a good lover too, quiet and affectionate and immune to the bigger feelings. He looks like it's easy to make him happy, but just as easy to make him sad. She envies his wife. Is he even married? In any event, a guy like that doesn't need a wife before fifty, and then just so he won't spend too much time alone.

A couple of times after her trips to Tegel she has gone back into town with a stranger. She didn't get on the express bus but into a taxi with the stranger to some hotel or other. There she'd have another drink at the bar, a whisky or two, until the desire to get closer than the edge of the breath went silent. At least for her. The rule is simple. Desire comes from nothing. When she refuses to pay it any attention, it disappears as unpredictably and quickly as it arrived. The older she gets the easier it gets to stick to the rule. And so, up till now, such evenings have always ended with a one-nil to her and no extra time stretching into the night.

I'm on the last flight to Moscow, he says, taking off his jacket and draping it over the back of the barstool. Tomorrow morning at six I have to keep on going, a domestic flight to Vladivostok, then on to Novosibirsk and Khabarovsk. Saturday morning I'll be back . . .

. . . from Khabarovsk, near China? she asks. They say that all the women there are business students and that they wear really tight skirts, is that true? She looks at the whorl of hair above his forehead, his eyes, his dark eyelashes, and once more at his hands. There was a time when she would fall in love with men despite their ugly hands, for they could walk on them. When he stands up, her eyes scan his jacket for dog hair.

Can you walk on your hands? she asks when he returns with a small beer for her and a large one for himself.

No, I'm too old for that kind of stuff.

How old are you then?

Thirty-six, and you?

My birthday's tomorrow, she says. A flat-out lie.

He smiles and watches a woman in a thin grey coat walk past, until she disappears by the exit of Terminal C.

And what's your name? he asks and looks at her as if torn from a dream.

Me?

Your name's Me?

He brushes a hand across the seat of his stool before sitting down. In the moment he was away a bunch of noisy little birds gathered in the empty space.

I don't walk on my hands, he says, but as a skilled German professional I use them to install compressors which are said to be the best in the world. I travel from oil refinery to oil refinery. Recently I've spent more and more time in Khabarovsk, always in the same hotel, with a view onto the Amur.

The River Amur?

Yeah.

She looks towards the exit of Terminal C, where the woman in the thin grey coat disappeared.

Do you like to be in the hotel there?

Yeah.

And the country, what's it like?

Dirt, dust, crap on gold, and sometimes marble. No doubt you're surprised as to why a German engineer is speaking this way, right? The thing about dirt, dust, crap, gold and marble is something my colleague Sergei always says. Our country's rotting, he says, the system's rotting. As for me, I'm always relieved when Friday comes round. Saturdays I fly back, but Fridays Sergei takes me to his weekend get-togethers with his friends. We sit in a garage, drink beer and vodka, someone plays guitar. The others laugh and sing along. I do too. Often, the mechanics who back in the GDR days would come to Khabarovsk can't speak any English. They've forgotten all their Russian. That's why Tatiana, Sergei's wife, is there, to act as an interpreter. He pauses before adding, Tatiana cries pretty easily and teaches yoga, too.

Does she like to wear a thin grey coat? she would like to ask.

The other day Tatiana fell off her chair at the end of one of our garage evenings, just like that. Not because she'd had too much vodka, but because she was exhausted, he says. You've got to be prepared for anything over there, and I am. Over there I'm prepared for anything. I could fall off my chair one day, too.

His mobile rings.

He stands up and takes a few steps away from the table. She watches him. My God, what kind of childhood must he have had to not have that relaxed way of moving suppressed and to give him that happy ease with which in no time at all he had caused that flutter of her heart and head, and of which he wasn't even aware? What is his presence reminding her of? That she was once capable of falling in love? And if so, what would that change now?

Across from the cafe a young saleswoman with a tired face was jerking a garment rack with twinsets back into place in front of her high-end shop until it was parallel with the window. Purple, she sees, is still available in any size. As far as red is concerned, however, there's just a single piece left, all the way to the front. Wasn't there once a kiosk for newspapers, postcards and see-through children's umbrellas instead of a boutique? Once, when was that?

The man had left his wallet lying next to his beer glass. The edge of a business card was peeking out of the pocket reserved for bills. She pulls it out with a jerk.

Storm, it says, Robert Storm.

I know that name, she thinks, I know the name Storm. But who hadn't known someone named Storm at some point? She glances over at him. He was still on the phone, his back was turned, and he was rocking back and forth from his knees. Was his wife or one of his kids on the other end of the line? How old would they be? Two girls with sharp faces and dimples? Or two boys who constantly hit each other because the little house, a rowhouse at the end of the street, was too small for four people and a dog? What made her think he lived in a little end rowhouse?

She stuffs the business card into her pocket.

Half an hour later he gets on his flight, and she takes the bus into town earlier than usual. Outside, it is August. Vladivostok, Khabarovsk, Novosibirsk. The city names combine into a rhythm that matches the movements of the bus. Vladi-Vostok-Kha-ba-rovsk-Novo-sibirsk, he would be landing at Tegel again the following Saturday. She pulls the business card out of her pocket. The address of his compressor business was printed in bold on the front, and on the back, small and in cursive, his private one. The bus bounced and buckled on through the early twilight.

. . . Storm, Robert Storm! *Only this one thing was plain, he was never seen again* . . . How did that line get into her head? From memory? From what had been forgotten? Whatever, the two things went together like yeast and dough. She leans her head against the glass. Once the bus is driving down a wide street like a flight path leading away from a canal she bends her back, pulls her head between her shoulders and tries to see as much sky as possible from her seat.

. . . *Soon they got to such height, they were nearly out of sight! And the hat went up so high, it almost touched the sky* . . .

## 30.12

The plan: When she's eighteen, she'll fall in love with a man who's thirty-six. When she's thirty-six, she'll in love with a man who's also thirty-six. When she's fifty-four, she'll fall in love with a man who, once again, is thirty-six. I know that much, I'm the narrator here.

The men remain thirty-six.

But what does she remain?


## 1.1

Told a man at a New Year's party yesterday that I once looked on as a girlfriend of mine squatted in a building until I eventually threw a stone myself. His comment: And back then I drove an Opel Kadett.

What colour?

Poppy-red.

What year was it built?

Sixty-three, he said, like me.

And: only just now on a bench with him in the Tiergarten, the man who once drove an Opel Kadett and still smokes. Beneath the bench an empty bottle of Rotkäppchen Sekt and the spent cartridges of a blank gun. He kicks one of the cartridges onto the path, without looking at me but into the sun, as if he were still waiting for someone, and says, In a boxing match those who fight back don't go crazy.

Do you box?

Yeah.

Crazy, I say.

And: What should the woman from the airport actually be called? Irmgard? Not at all? Nina? Nope.
Konstanze? No. Laura? Maybe . . . that might work.

Like me?

Me?


## 31.1

Would you like to help me come up with a ballet?

For?

A couple of elephants.

How old?

Really young.

(*Pause.*)

The Opel Kadett driver from before, who now
drives a Volvo, leans against my fridge and says,
OK, if the elephants are really young, I'll do
it.

MONDAY

She places a box of teabags on the table and looks at the label. English Breakfast. My God, how long she's been in Berlin already! This life of hers had slowly grown up around her, become familiar, and there's really nothing much to see that you couldn't have seen hours, days, years before. She'd come here at the beginning of the '80s with two suitcases and the train, back when taking a train to West Berlin wasn't just a simple here-to-there with the high-speed ICE, but a long trip on green or red imitation-leather seats, with scraped armrests between each person. In winter, with the appearance of the border guards, the heating regularly stopped so that more than once in the middle of the Cold War she'd almost frozen to death thanks to German–German relations. She takes two bags out of the box and pours water over them. She remembers. The first time she was in Berlin was with Nina, on a school trip. At the border the girls grew quiet. The boys all turned into James Bonds behind mirrored sunglasses. GDR border guards moved from compartment to compartment with vendor trays of transit visas, stamped the papers for the fluffy kids from the West in their velour pullovers, those kids who had learnt that throughout the entire Zone there weren't any sardines, no whole asparagus spears, just the bottoms. The asparagus tips were exported from an illegitimate country that went by the name of the German Democratic Republic to the West. I don't buy it, Nina had said, there's no way. On the second day of their trip Nina and she had taken the U-Bahn alone over to Wedding. They sat at the window, for there was something to see: underground ghost stations in the eastern half of the city, where the train did not stop but went more slowly. Mounds of coal had been dumped in front of the exits leading upstairs. Placards outside of little Mitropa kiosks announced the victory of the people's revolution or an international football match in Walter Ulbricht Stadium. People's revolution, Nina had said, the way you repeat a foreign word you want to ingrain in your mind and pointed to the soldiers standing under the emergency lighting which reflected green off the green-tiled walls. Had they got lost in the darkened corridors of their own lives? Were these ghost stations simply echoes from the void? That just can't be, Nina had said, and on the last day of their trip they had gone over to East Berlin to see what the world above the ghost stations looked like. At the Tränenpalast border crossing they were caught by a sudden shower which threw a thin curtain across the yellow headlamps of the Trabis, Ladas and Wartburgs and over the streets. Unter den Linden didn't smell like linden trees at all, but like exhaust, and in a milk bar at Alexanderplatz, called Ice Bear or Espressobar, two boys—their fingers raised in Vs and barely any older than Nina or her, wearing stonewashed jeans and blue-tinted glasses—edged their way into the photo in which, later on, they all looked like they'd been scared by a snake. Or was it the memory that later, in its own way, illuminated the film as well? She takes the two teabags out of the pot. What had the name of that old national railway disinfectant been? Without a doubt the leftover stock was sold in Ukraine, or even further east. During the train ride that smell had settled in to their hair and clothing like the smell of old pea soup. North Koreans probably smelt that way now. But she'd forgotten what the stuff was called. Whatever. She fishes her breakfast egg out of the boiling water and toasts two slices of white bread. What had the name of her professor for philosophical foundations of psychiatry and psychotherapy been? Him, the one who during his lectures would like to repeat a single phrase and then look up from his manuscript while letting the phrase grow larger in the stillness of the lecture hall . . . We are what we have forgotten.

But what was the professor's name? Weißbach?

She puts the white bread on a plate and throws away the package of cream cheese. It has mould. She cleans the salad spinner and dries it off. When she goes to turn the handle, it gets stuck. Oh man, Johann, she thinks, but that man who could have solved the problem with his big, skilled hands is no longer a part of her life.

Kiss me, she'd said to the man her friend, Nina, had introduced her to as Johann. That New Year's Eve she closed her eyes as his breath, his lips, his chest, his heartbeat touched her. Behind her eyelids the whirling of leaves. Every leaf, a laugh. She, a medical doctor without any real job, was thirty-six years old, had been in Berlin for eighteen years and separated from Viktor for three. Numbers told stories. Hers did, too. More and more fireworks shot into the air. In no more than five minutes the sky would be a smoky, dirty yellow. But in the end it was only a motion detector at the edge of a moss-covered stone terrace in Pankow that tore her and that Johann out of the darkness of the garden, shortly after midnight. What a dumb light it was, crying out at each and every cat and rat. The moment it flicked on they continued to cling to each other as if even the minutest change

17

between them would toss them off the edge of the terrace, the edge of the world. A new year and a new millennium had begun.

She'd come back to Berlin on a train from the edge of the Ruhr district in the early afternoon and in a bad mood. The days between the years on the eighth floor with her mother and grandmother had been marked by an evil-grey eternity and had triggered a hopelessness she knew well from before. Boredom. If it'd been summer, she would have retreated to the balcony under the shadow of the satellite dish, and would have been able to correct the 'Shores of Consciousness' manuscript for a scientific publishing house she was working for as a freelancer. But holing up with the pile of papers she'd brought with her in the overheated living room was hopeless. A lot of things were hopeless there, where she came from.

Arrival. Track 3.

Bahnhof Zoo Station had four tracks and, therefore, was no bigger than any old station off in the sticks. Don't come too late, Nina had said, that way you can still be a part of our action. She took the suburban rail people called the S-Bahn and got off near Hackescher Markt for the tram. Our action, Nina had said, starts there and stretches out over the next three or four stops.

Once the tram got moving, a young woman abruptly stood up. She had a wide cat-like face and walked to the front of the car to press the stop button next to the driver. Milk spilling out of her shopping bag. Don't you see any thing? an old man asked. Turning away from him the woman with the cat's face said, No. She got off at the next stop while a bunch of children pushed their way past her into the tram, five of them squeezing themselves into a seat made for four until a girl elbowed the boy next to her: Come on, man, go somewhere else. The boy stood up and hung off the strap with one hand. Milk spilling out of his back-pack. Everyone saw it, but no one said a thing. She didn't either. At the next stop the kids got off. The man who now got on was thirty-six, as old as she was, she learnt later, and was wearing a tattered tote bag over his shoulder, which didn't suit him at all. He sat down across from her and looked into her eyes. She returned his gaze. He reached into the bag. Puckered his lips. They broke into a smile, a bit unsure maybe, a bit melancholic, but then got stuck halfway.

The tram kept on going.

Kiss me, she thought.

Kiss me or throw me against the wall, his glance replied before he got up and walked down the car. Milk spilling out of his tote bag. Hey! the old man called out. Hey! What's all this about? What's your name? His fingers spread out as if ready to wrestle, he stood up and with a few wide-legged steps placed himself right in front of the man with the tote bag, who for his part just sunk his head and smiled his unfinished smile from the other side. I've forgotten it, he said casually and beatifically.

My God, is he friendly, she thought.

Nina was waiting at the next stop with a sign that had been painted with the question that was also the title of their action: How Many Outrageous Things Do I Resign Myself to Every Day?

Once the tram had begun to move again Nina raised her sign even higher. Nina, her friend from before, the little girl from the other side of the abandoned lot where her parent's yellow villa stood, pouring honey into the night with the warm light of its windows, while over at theirs, up on the eighth floor, there was a TV-quiz show turned up far too loud, her mother whinnying on the worn-out sofa next to her grandmother, opening another bottle of beer, and her, leaning out over the concrete railing. Plagued by feelings of emptiness . . .

Then the man with the tote bag walked up and stood next to Nina. Their shoulders touched as he lit his cigarette.

They need to get real jobs, the old man said, spreading all ten of his fingers against the glass as they passed.

Someone should shoot every last one of them!

The man with the tote bag was named Johann, he worked in the theatre, but not onstage. Sadly, he said. That stated, the most important things in his life didn't have to do with art, but football, bicycles and women. And so, on that New Year's Eve, he reacquainted himself with an old question.

Why didn't I become a teacher? An unglamorous but secure existence, no doubt.

Thirty-six's a bit late for those kinds of doubts, don't you think? she replied. What do you do in the theatre?

I'm a dramaturge. There was something decisively un-depressing about him when he said that.

What exactly does a dramaturge do?

With her question she lured him away from the party that Nina had brought them both to, lured him onto the moss-covered stone terrace, out into the cold, the open air, where they were alone. The others inside the house were gathered around a tray with glasses of Sekt and began the countdown in loud voices as outside she said, Kiss me, you don't love your girlfriend any more anyway.

Which girlfriend?

Didn't you come here with Nina?

You did too. Have you all known each other for a long time?

Have you?

Then he kissed her, but it was far too short due to that damn motion detector, and Nina was standing inside by the panorama window, her hands in the pockets of her wide trousers, her white men's shirt buttoned all the way up to the top. Nina, the flick knife, next to whom she'd always felt like an old rubber. Nina, charming, bright, derisive and most of the time unemployed, when she wasn't launching a milk action like the one earlier that afternoon, that is.

When the new millennium was still rather young, she and Johann went back into the house as if nothing had happened and danced in a circle with all the others to 'Zehn kleine Jäger-meister' by the Toten Hosen. Afterwards they pushed up against each other in a corner, where she ripped open the sewn pockets of his new, pike-grey suit in order to bury her hands, her shame-less joy inside them.

By that time Nina had already left.

Although the streets on that New Year's Eve of 1999 were slick with ice, from one moment to the next she'd decided to cycle home. Johann and she, however, had danced until the morning of the new millennium instead. Around five they went back to his place. He had undressed her solemnly: Be still, Beau-tiful. Shortly after seven she had looked at the luminous num-bers of the clock next to his bed, while they lay next to each other, naked, and she balanced an ashtray on her stomach, its cool metal telling the story of how the last few hours had felt. Johann stubbed out his cigarette. You don't need to do that, she said, but she liked it.

Would she ever learn at how many tables and after how many Jägermeisters which version of this story Nina would tell?

Or would Nina simply forget the evening and her body alone remember him as she rode home alone across the mirror-smooth streets?

On one of the following nights she dreamt that she was jogging through a hilly area, wearing a winter coat with side pockets as big as saddlebags: I've got a bunch of dead animals inside, would you be so kind as to pull them out? she asked those she encountered. Ask Johann, they all replied. Over and over she asked, and over and over she received the same answer: Ask Johann. Finally she posed a different question: Who's Johann?

... and the world exploded.

The got married one year later.

No, they did not get married.

Monday morning. She places the salad spinner next to the bin bag by the front door, walks to the bathroom but doesn't put on the jeans or the blouse hanging over the heater. Only next Saturday. She takes the business card out of the back pocket and balances it on the washbasin, against the toothbrush glass.

Robert Storm. *Only this one thing was plain, he was never seen again...*

The name smiled at her mysteriously. But he had a totally normal address: No. 7 Schenkendorfstraße, Berlin Kreuzberg, a fax machine and a phone, and he could be reached by mobile too. The mirror behind the toothbrush glass opened like a window onto a second room where none of that existed but at the same time it all repeated. It is snowing. Those are tiny splotches of toothpaste on the glass. Those are the flakes driving Robert Storm on alone through Vladivostok, Khabarovsk, Novosibirsk, past shops with dark windows and even darker rooms behind them, but windows which nevertheless allow the silhouettes of people to be seen, people who, in an eternal, eastern twilight, are going on with their lives or simply sitting, talking, smoking and showing him, Storm, the way down to the Amur, the river that, in such weather, is no longer a river but a glimmering white, deeply frozen road strewn with cars and fishermen leaning against their driver-side doors. Small, bloody bait fish twitching at their feet at the edge of the black holes they've drilled into the ice. Yes, the holes are black, the snow is white and the fish's blood is red in that wintry Siberian fairy tale in which she is now walking next to Storm, away from the Amur and along the promenade, and he has opened an umbrella to hold above them until they reach a bar and stop and he closes it again, and deposits it in a corner where a dog is sleeping, curled up. In the dim light between the loud, Russian-speaking drunks she quickly reapplies her lipstick then huddles up next to Storm, the only quiet face in the room, who now turns to her for coming in too close with a bit of a sneer but is glad at the same time. My God, what wonderful spots he has on his face, which some god or other has sown there so that he will only harvest joy! Spots like splotches of toothpaste, but not white, rather a colour similar to café-au-lait. His voice gives the impression that he could sing well when he says, My umbrella there, did you notice, it is indeed black, but it's a children's umbrella and too small to protect two people. But whatever, there's music. They begin to dance all the way through the room and out the back door. It leads to a dark courtyard. They keep on dancing all the way to an off-road vehicle whose window is being covered in flakes. She wipes them away.

They drive off.

Where are they headed?

No one can say.

With the bin bag and the broken salad spinner under her arm (which disappears into a recycling bin), she leaves her house half an hour later and makes her way to the hairdresser's. It's her day off.

Is the water OK?

What do you mean?

Sometimes people complain, they say that the temperature goes back and forth.

People, she says, what can you do? She is the only client, maybe because it's a Monday. Already on the way here she had been happy thinking about the concentration with which he would massage the shampoo and conditioner into her wet hair, that pleasantly anonymous tenderness spreading out through the one-and-a-half kilo, 37-degree bit of biomass beneath her skull. How often he had already scared away those dark birds wanting to build nests in her hair. Washing out the special rinse for strawberry blondes he too repeats: People, what can you do? She leans her head further back, closes her eyes and says, Hardly anyone knows people better than you, running through your course of washing-haircutting-talking every day as you do. Go on and let them talk, for that's all there is.

You think?

They talk about brain research like it's a new religion, too.

Really?

The hairdresser drops a comb. He bends over. When he straightens back up, laboriously but with a smile, it looks as if he's slipped a disc.

He grabs a fire-engine red hand towel.

A turban like this suits you well, you're a silent beauty, that's why you can get away with something this flashy, he observes, guiding her over to the mirror, where she sits down and he wraps the towel more tightly above her forehead.

Coffee or water, Doctor?

Both, please.

He disappears into his cubbyhole behind the register, where a machine begins to buzz as it makes a drip coffee, just like when she was in the department of neurosurgery. It always tasted stale, even when it had just been prepared for those morning meetings behind the drawn curtains, bathed in the play of light of a seven o' clock sun. In the warm months she'd climbed on to the roof of the building opposite. Outside construction on the courtyard was getting underway, which was why, inside, one of the tired people in white had shut the tilted window to better understand the assistant physician, a Hungarian woman, sitting on top of the rubbish bin, coffee cup in hand, giving reports on the previous night's arrivals: female polytrauma, born 1964, brought in around twelve thirty, fell from the seventh floor onto the flowerbed in front of her building after fighting with a friend. Fracture of the central skull and methadone. She's in the room next to our complicated old guy, the one who smells of urine. At those moments someone in the station briefing room had always laughed tiredly . . .

Milk, sugar? the hairdresser calls out from his cubbyhole.

Both, please, she says, and her mobile in front of the mirror shows it's shortly after four.

She is fifty-four.


I think that you'll be even more beautiful when you get older, Beautiful, Johann had said three months after that New Year's Eve in which not only the year but the millennium had changed. On that day at the end of March they had driven out of the city and stopped at a restaurant, but not gone inside. They were both thirty-six. They sat on the bonnet of an old white Mercedes, smoking and looking ever-deeper into the landscape. He didn't speak. But it didn't matter; his presence was enough. The sky above them was a deep blue. Just like the sea, she thought. For the first time in her life she had the desire to describe the afternoon, nothing but the afternoon. She wasn't a born storyteller, that much was clear. Nina perhaps, but not her.

Be that as it may, you were still allowed to write without writing, right?

She looked at Johann. His gaze was once again as barefoot as it had been a few weeks ago in the tram, shortly before the milk had begun to spill out of his tote. She wove herself into that distant gaze, which hung like a thread from her memory. Her grandmother, for example, who, working for 398 marks a month sewing mattresses on the assembly line, gave her a thousand marks when she finished school saying, Make something of it, then cried, which was why she turned to face the cupboard in the tiny kitchen on the eighth floor and make them both a piece of bread with artificial honey. With a cigarette in the corner of her mouth and only a few dyed strands of hair on her head. Her grandmother belonged in the feeling of that moment, and was sitting on the bonnet of the white Mercedes together with them, out of place, but welcome.

Do you remember the apple tree, the one from back then? she asks. Do you recognize it when you look at the metal of the bonnet between you and this man? You're reflecting each other there, the two of you, and the apple tree's there too, the one you used to sit under for days, in your pushchair, kicking against the undersides of its leaves. Their bright bellies. If someone had asked you, back then, you would have toothlessly and happily said on record that the world was a friendly and warm place.

Even when staring straight ahead. Do you remember? And tell me, studying the brain, did you ever figure out where your memories go when you don't have them? Or where the memory of this man who's sitting beside you will be one day, this man who's lighting a cigarette with a lighter whose sharp click-clack will become the tuning fork of this successful afternoon? Where will the memory of this afternoon be once you've forgotten it? And where will those of this man next to you be once he's gone? You could tell him now, as long as your afternoon is still pure presence, about the good marks you got on your graduation exams, about your fear of failure and about the mole on your groin, the one on the left, the one you should keep an eye on. Yes, someone should definitely keep an eye on it, and on you as well, her grandmother says with her voice of glass.

Happiness and glass, how easily both of them break . . .

Should I give you a compliment? Johann had asked at that moment.

Yes.

I love you, Beautiful.

He placed a foot on the bumper and looked like a cowboy, even if he didn't have the right boots. Afterwards they both continued to look out into the landscape, which faded into a vague blur. What a place, the clouds moving by with the slow speed of the earth. She noticed that she was already familiar with everything there, even if she'd forgotten where she had once seen it all, had experienced it all, and had even had that very same thought: the thought that she had once had that very same thought. And that the bonnet of the old white Mercedes wasn't a memory, or just the memory of an earlier memory. Even the man next to her wasn't a case of déjà vu. No. He and the memories were what they were. Life.

Later, on the search for moments in her past that she would only have to think back in order to understand her present, she would remember that afternoon on the bonnet.

Again the question: They got married a year later?

No, they did not get married.

The following year, however, they moved to the Rhine together. With a temporary position she left Berlin behind, where she had lived for eighteen years, at first with, then without Viktor.

Johann followed from Magdeburg, at first with, then without a car.

His offices grew smaller and smaller from job to job. As did the theatres where he worked. At the beginning he'd stayed in one theatre for years. Later on, his dramaturgical contracts would be limited to two or three years and never extended.

You've got to keep on going, he said, just keep on going, there are those that wander and those that sit on the couch.

But did a wanderer always choose to hardly ever be settled?

Goddamn rootless—Johann's friends who'd stayed behind in the city he'd left would say. For his part, Johann simply found his old friends old.

What am I supposed to do with roots when I can't take them with me, Beautiful?

His next-to-last office at the theatre of Dresden had been under the roof, next to the men's toilet, and he'd had to share his last one at the Kammerspiele Magdeburg with a younger colleague. Good guy, Beautiful, a smoker too.

Had he also called Nina 'Beautiful'?

Johann had managed to be dismissed from Magdeburg through a discrete and friendly refusal to work. Now he was unemployed. They threw their lives together all the more determinedly and moved to the Rhine. Whether they would make it there remained unclear, though the fact that they liked each other in a considerate way did not.

Nina was never discussed.

Following the removal van out of Magdeburg in the white Mercedes, not far from the former border, under an Autobahn bridge, there was a bang like a deadly explosion. Immediately thereafter the motor went kaput. They got out. Johann opened the bonnet. They looked out into the landscape, which disappeared together with the Elbe into a vague blur, treeless, cloudless and as if fleeing from itself. What a place, she said dreamily, placing her hand at the very base of his back while he shook his head above the engine. Right, take your hand off my ass, Johann said, we've got other problems at the moment. The engine block is done. I forgot to fill up the coolant.

She looked out into the landscape alone. What a beautiful, friendly, attentive person, she'd thought up till now. Of course, he probably still was beautiful, friendly and attentive, she just didn't see it at the moment any longer. The car upon whose bonnet they had once remained for an entire afternoon—even if only in the desire to be—would now have to be scrapped. The towing service arrived. Two very blond men with red faces jumped out of the cab and extended a hand to Johann alone. We'll hang a photo of it in a silver frame in our new flat, she said a few hundred metres later as the trailer with the white Mercedes disappeared. Instead of answering, Johann laughed. It sounded like defiant trumpeting.

Damn it, why, just as they were moving in together, did she no longer really see them together?

Their first night there they slept on unfolded moving boxes. This isn't a flat, it's a hole, Johann said, casting his eyes at the ceiling as if early the next morning already instead of a lamp he wanted to install a hook and on the hook a rope and on the rope himself. But he wasn't like that. A rope was a rope, a hook was a hook. Johann wasn't one of those people who abused things. OK, he said instead when getting up, let me be the man of the house, Beautiful. He took a hook and a cord, hung up his old Japanese lantern, and was happy with the red lacquered-wood wall cabinet she'd bought in the early '80s in Berlin. She'd been eighteen. Then Johann mounted the cupboard above the former tenant's sink. Whenever life got difficult Johann would begin making things, as if in doing so any other damages would be repaired at the same time. Soon she would be asking herself why he had never opened a bicycle repair shop and given so much of his life to other people and—for him, maybe even the wrong place— the theatre instead.

What do you do? What's the name of your scientific project again? I didn't really understand it during our first conversation on the phone. How, oh, I see, you conduct medically based emotional perception tests? On people? And your husband, what does he do again? Sorry, a dramaturge, that's something like a doctor, right?

She hadn't wanted to disagree with their soon-to-be land-lord. He was a chipper Rhinelander who only really cared about the world so long as it came down the street dressed as a carnival float. If he understood Johann's job as a dramaturge to be an obscure part of skin medicine, well, so be it, the important thing was getting the flat, which Johann would grow used to for the simple fact that she liked it. Downstairs at the entrance there was a red light, which gave the building behind the station an unserious air. But so what, she was a life scientist. In Berlin she'd lived above a brothel for years, second floor, back courtyard on the left, stove heating and a small balcony like a stone nest stuck out over the rubbish bins down below, which did a poor job of concealing the branches of a frail sycamore tree. Sometimes an empty plastic bag would get caught in the limbs. Around noon the brothel in the front building would open two of its windows to let in a bit of air. The cleaning woman's humming would drift out into the courtyard. The club was a favourite of lorry drivers, especially the ones that liked to wear women's clothes. They'd handed over their coal cellar to the woman from the fourth floor. It had been turned into a dominatrix studio, and her upstairs neighbour would go to work with her Alsatian. Always. Sometimes when going down the linoleum stairs it would start to slide, its nails making a noise that said: This is what it's like when you're old. You're old when you're about to die. Coming home one night she caught two men pissing in the front hall by the letterboxes. She laughed and said, No worries, gentlemen, carry on. I'm a doctor.

The two rooms there along the Rhine were on the first floor, above a nightclub, near the main train station, but far from sanitized areas like the old city or the port. From the outside the building looked respectable with its expensive tiles, but the soot was deep down in the stone. The ground floor only came to life at weekends. A couple of sad solo shows by old cabaretists or a semi-professional chanteuse, accompanied by her husband on piano, presenting songs by Juliette Gréco, Barbara or Dalida. Can I tell you something, Johann? she said shortly after moving in. This is exactly how I always imagined artists to live.

Johann smiled, And how is that? He seemed to have had enough of art. Or of her?

The hallway smells of mould, Beautiful.

Better than piss.

At night you can hear the trains.

There's something about it.

What, may I ask?

Something tender.

Don't get all kitschy, he said, lighting a cigarette.

They lived on a street where shoes were resoled, and bicycles repaired. The first time she'd come there to see the flat was on a Sunday and she'd been alone. She liked the street's atmosphere. Everything felt kind of leftover, particularly the lime-green sheets in a dusty shop window, next to which there was a red chewing gum dispenser with a handle. That afternoon the sun had shone down on the pavement, empty parking spaces and flat, mortared garages with a particularly Sunday kind of brightness that made her feel like she was living in an important dream. Her life could turn out OK again. If I were to look into a mirror, she thought, I'd see a woman living way back in time, like a woman in a painting, with curtains hanging loosely to the floor in folds behind her.

Johann had not come with her that Sunday. That's why he was not in the dream.

The hairdresser comes back with coffee, milk, sugar, biscuits and water, and places everything in front of the mirror where, in a silver stand, he keeps his business cards. He pulls a stool over to sit right behind her and begins to part her wet hair with a comb.

You're a special person, I could see that the very first time I came here.

Thank you, he says, that's nice of you to say, but I'm afraid I'm going to have to disappoint you. I'm not that special at all.

Are you sure?

Totally. For example, that thing about brain research and religion, what you just said, I didn't understand a thing.

We'll do it together—Putamen Amen, she says.

Sorry?

She takes the comb from his hand and rasps its teeth in her wet hair around her fontanelle.

The putamen, she says, is right in the middle of the core of my grey matter. It coordinates movement and makes it difficult for me to stumble around all the time. Amen. Here, she continues, moving in an elegant comb-curve in the direction of her forehead, here in the limbic system is where love and hate live.

The hairdresser gulps. Not in the heart, Doctor?

Just a moment, I'm not done yet. Mind and memory are located in the hippocampus, right here, she reaches for his hand and places his fingers on her temples.

And melancholy, where is melancholy located, Doctor? The hairdresser pulls his fingers back.

Well, melancholy . . .

With the comb she traces a line from ear to ear, like a pair of headphones.

A lot of melancholy or depression sits right here on the right, in the cerebral cortex, she says, whereas mathematics, speech and intelligence are on the left. That would be the first rough sketch of the twists and turns of the brain, she continues, but don't think that that alone makes a person. If everything that a person is was just the mass of his or her brain, then the taste of a strawberry, the painfulness of your pain, the smell of your wet dog and countless other impressions—not to mention faith, love and hope—would lose their power, they would simply be

33

the electrical signals of the organ beneath your skull, which is the colour of semolina porridge.

The hairdresser's glance in the mirror says, No way.

It's true, she says, whoosh! That's how quickly it can go, that's how quickly a person can become a brain-ality instead of a person-ality.

No, the hairdresser says, that doesn't just happen with a whoosh.

It does, she reasons, and a person can even take medicine to counteract their shyness.

No, the hairdresser says dismissively, that's not a person any more.

They are, she says.

Seriously?

Seriously would be a good name for a person, she laughs.

The hairdresser takes the comb out of her hand and begins to pull the wet ends of her hair straight, with a concentrated look.

Who'd want something like that, he asks, I mean, where's free will?

When half an hour later she turns around again by the bus stop on the corner, the hairdresser is standing in the doorway of his shop, eating a banana. Schenkendorfstraße, he'd said as she was paying, you can get the bus there on the corner every ten minutes. The street's real close to that old cemetery in Kreuzberg, where my father's buried too. Tell me, you doing all right?

Why?

You look so different today.

That's got everything to do with you, *meister*.

The woman was responsible for me as well, Johann had said once they'd been living together for two or three months above the nightclub. I liked her dimples, and she wasn't too far off with her predictions. She'd seen right away that it'd be tough to place me. Same thing with that guy there maybe.

He pushed the newspaper over to her, past the bowl of risotto. Outside the rain slid quickly down the window. A fifty-two-year-old unemployed man with a heavy and tired face had shot the young woman with dimples during a consultation meeting, the caption under the photo reported.

I hope she didn't have any children. Johann, how old was she?

About as old as we are. Thirty-six, perhaps.

Awful.

It's worse than that, Johann said, it's a real goddamn mess.

He got up from the kitchen table and tossed the paper with the murderer into the bin, walked into the hall and pulled a notebook out of one of the cartons, which were still in the corridor, next to the wardrobe. Basement books, he called them, and they'd probably stay in those cartons for ever.

He disappeared into his room, came back, poured himself a whisky and, glass in hand, looked at her silently, gently, before disappearing a second time. He didn't close the door behind him completely. I guess you'll probably go find a job when you no longer have any money for cigarettes and booze, she called after him. In the hallway she heard his Zippo click. Then he stuck his head through the door again.

Turn on the radio to keep yourself company, Beautiful, he said.

At that moment she saw herself through his eyes, sitting there, at the table. She didn't have a hardy face, but more of a night face, which might've had to do with the fact that she didn't sleep well. Was that also where her bedroom eyes, as her mother called them, came from? The Mona Lisa also had bedroom eyes. Was that why her smile was so difficult to explain? She'd once read how the experts had examined the pigment structure of the painting, in vain. The mystery of the spirit, the woman's being, had remained. In any event, an actress who was curious or sad, or had a similar disposition or look on her face could train herself to have that very same smile in order to finally say what a woman with just such a look on her face was capable of. On horseback and with an axe. But did she really want to know?

Do I really want to know? she'd asked herself, in the meantime, thirty-seven and a doctor without any steady employment.

Become a doctor, a psychiatrist, Nina had said during their last year at school.

When she was right, she was right. On top of it, the excitement with which her friend had made the recommendation was infectious. As opposed to Nina she'd always grown bored during their six-hour maths class and, by the first break, as opposed to all the others in the class as well, she'd already be finished. Boredom comes from stupidity; she'd been convinced of that much even back then. And her absolutely sensational 0.9 average didn't change that opinion. At their graduation party, Nina and she had got drunk and taken off their shoes to dance, which in that grey, enshrouded valley at the edge of the Ruhr was akin to something like a striptease. Was boredom a feeling or a state? And were all feelings simply signals from the brain? She asked her biology teacher during a slow waltz. He answered with some formula or formulaic phrase or other, which she forgot as soon as she heard it. While sucking on a violet-flavoured lozenge, he could not say whether a person was their brain or something more. Whether what a person thought was also what they felt. Whether at the end of a life there was something like a recountable narrative or whether the memory of each and every human being lied in conjunction with the larger and smaller lies of their life. Due to the fact that despite getting good marks she did not have a talent for anything in particular, she decided to study medicine. She followed Nina's inner voice. Not her own. She was diligent, could think quickly, and wanted to push her own, small but secure life between herself and where she came from. Had she had a talent for playing football or dancing, she might've chosen a different path. But talent was nothing other than interest, and she enjoyed using her brain to think about her brain. She enjoyed paradoxical situations that could not be solved with effort, but only withstood. When later on in her studies she began to research her own brain—that furrowed, walnut-like, porridge-grey clump of protein, carbohydrates and fat—in order to understand more about the being of the brain, to spend entire nights in books before ending up stuck between scientific discoveries and completely different, unsettling questions that far too often had to do with a man named Viktor who was eighteen years older than she was, that in-between, that no-man's-land continued to have the scent of violet-flavoured lozenges even years after their graduation party. Financed by the state as well as her own pockets she finished her studies slowly. The reason it took longer than usual didn't just have to do with Viktor but also a huge fear of future patients, whom she, as a doctor, wouldn't be able to endure. She had never really believed that her hands were intelligent enough to operate on a brain. In the end, just the thought of a career in medicine and its attendant social climbing made her tired, apathetic. Whenever someone asked her how she was, she would begin to yawn, even when she wasn't tired. During her intern year she spent her time in neurosurgery with a crazy professor who did everything because the good Lord wanted it that way. He spurred him on. Not her. During the doctorial colloquiums she continued to attend every week in order to remain a student within the safe space of the university, she would smile into the faces of the other young doctors. Emotional contagion of the healthy and the mentally ill.

Over and over, every third Wednesday of the month she would present the arduous progress of her work to the same work circle. The always-the-same must be the best part, Viktor had said. Was he right? Her listeners just stared back at her impassively. But when had she begun to find the others shift-less? If anyone was shiftless there, if anyone just let life do what it had to do, it was her. In any event, one day while they were standing next to the coffee machine a colleague of hers said, With this theme of yours you'd be better off in the theatre. Beneath the statement lay a second one: With this friend of yours, this Viktor, it'd be best to call it quits, he's far too old for you, take me instead! She walked past her colleague along the glass windows looking onto the courtyard of the university where a man in a blue apron, who was even older than Viktor, was trimming the boxwoods.

After the fall of the Wall, she got a job with a female GP who had additional training in psychotherapy but was clearly upset by the fact that she wasn't a proper psychiatrist. The office was ninety kilometres north of the centre city, in the direction of Rostock. She would ride there with the train. Viktor didn't like to lend her his car, and she didn't have one of her own. When her train was stopped in Löwenberg, by the little station garden a bunch of geese would stand side by side on an unpaved road, holding their heads in a way that suggested an incurable longing for nationally owned enterprises. Whenever a goose left the group and waddled up to the colourful iron fence of the platform to press its white chest against the bars, she would try to wave. At the following station young kids in green bomber jackets would be hanging around the only bench on the platform, all pale and like little flags of smoke. On a few of them, even from the distance, she recognized Veraguth's fold on their upper eyelids, a sign of depression. At the next stop black chickens picked about in dirty snow, at times in grey grass, and clearly lived in a dog kennel. Someone who had to be young and full of attainable dreams had arranged a cosy cluster of car seats on its roof. If she ever had a dog, that's the kind of living room it would have. She liked dogs. With dogs you could walk the streets alone and undisturbed, past people who ideated in a mature avocado beneath their skulls—on the results of the last vote, on bombings, imminent wars, American or other presidents, or on the death of glaciers. A dog didn't notice when, not having an opinion, she didn't have anything to add. And when she wasn't thinking about anything at all, the dog didn't notice that either. No, you can forget all about that, the GP with additional training in psychotherapy had said, a permanent position here is out of the question. You with your difficulties dealing with patients, what do you think, you can't even get a grip on the general day-to-day dealings of a GP office for me. On top of it, your neuroses and mine don't get along too well, do they? True, she said, and felt her shoulders grow tight. She gave notice the next day.

From that point on she kept afloat by working as a typist at her old university, where her doctoral advisor encouraged her to once and for all finish her dissertation on emotional infection. And so she crawled on, from chapter to chapter, from temporary contract to temporary contract, from evening to evening, with or without Viktor, until they broke up in 1996. Because of a woman. One of many and, truth be told, more of a birch than a woman, the one who Viktor, suddenly in need of the solace of trees, had brought with him from Moscow. The relationship just did not make any sense to her. Three years after their breakup, at the turn of the millennium, she finally had her PhD in her pocket but was convinced that, both as a doctor and in general, she was completely incompetent. She scraped together a living as a freelance editor for scientific publishing houses, editing manuscripts with titles like 'Decade of the Brain' or 'Who Is I' or 'The Shores of Consciousness'. And that's when the next man came along, in a white Mercedes, and took her to the Rhine.

Johann . . .

In the meantime, for almost ten years now, she has been working in Berlin again as a secretary in a neurobiological institute.

Without Johann.

And Nina? Her old friend had probably become a charming estate agent or was sitting behind a supermarket register or at an equestrian centre where men as well as women fell in love with her. Maybe she was going around giving interviews as a former punk rocker, with some of the old rage clearly still intact. Or maybe she'd ended up working for a crisis line or even for the ground crew of some airport or other. In any event, she continues to take her old friend into account, expressly when she's not doing that well. But her job at the institute is really nice. The street below her window is filled with lovely acacia trees, just like back on the street where she'd lived with Viktor. Sometimes one of the young biologists from the lab across the hall—Daniel, Raoul, Alasdair or whatever the young men around her were called—stops to stand in her office door and ask: How are you doing?

Hi, what can I do for you?

She looks up and slowly, very slowly pulls her hands away from her face. A Monday, shortly before six. First row, sundown, Berlin Kreuzberg. An old market hall, tastefully renovated, with a cafe at one end, its chairs turned towards the setting sun as if there was a beach beneath the stones. She'd just sat down at a free table. Next to the cafe, on the same side of the street, a post office. Between the post office and cafe a play park with climbing frames of brightly coloured wood for under-fourteens. On the benches by the fence four women, most likely mothers, with coffee cups in one last ray of sun and a fifth there too with a face so narrow that even from the front it looks like it does in profile. On the other side of the street an old woman with a rollator had stepped into the entrance with the words 'Trinity Cemetery' above it. The August sky above the inscription is deep blue, like the sea, as blank as a mirror, azure, glittering like a precious stone. It stretches out to all sides, immense and quiet, she desires to leap into it from her chair. The air is crisp, tinged with departure. Yes, she knows it won't be around much longer, the weather. It's a stroke of luck, a gift, an unexpected moment of serendipity, and Robert Storm lives around the corner.

Hello, would you like any thing now?

Did she? In reality, she was just fine. But if Storm were to ask her one day what she'd done with her life, what would she say? Would she just tell him? The dumbest stories make sense once they're told. No?

Are you alone, are you waiting on someone?

Being alone is bad for one's health, she knows that, and that's why women over thirty-six are often haunted by a fearful five minutes during the night. She was eighteen when she moved to Berlin and had bought the red lacquered-wood wall cabinet and some other used furniture for cheap here nearby,

41

close to Schenkendorfstraße, in one of those basement junk-shops for which the neighbourhood was known back then. She can still recall the smell of food from generations of renters nesting in the floors whenever she went to visit someone. She was from the provinces, had an unremarkable face if with eyes and a nose right where they belonged peering out from below a strawberry-blonde curtain of hair, parted in the middle. Without your curls you'd look like a barn owl, Viktor had said. By now her curls had disappeared. Viktor and the junkshops too, replaced by sushi and wok joints, Mongolian barbecue and a shop for dog collars. The first few weeks she was in Berlin, before she knew Viktor, she'd lived in a guesthouse beside Zoo Station and gone to buy the papers with flat-rental inserts on Sunday mornings at five until finding the offer for the place over in the Rote Insel area of Schöneberg. Surrounded by the S-Bahn tracks the people there lived with little money, workers, small-time employees, students. Hallways without any lights and places with stories about jazz musicians and left-wingers around the time of the November Revolution. The singer Marianne Rosenberg lived there, not far from the building where Marlene Dietrich had been born. By one of S-Bahn bridges there was a male nightingale who, in spring, would sing till morning. His arias made the night larger somehow, but he never found a mate. At the end of May, he simply went silent. The male nightingale remained childless. The corner bar was called To the Trough and had a jukebox. Mornings around five, after her late shift at the hospital where, in addition to her medical studies, she worked as an assistant nurse, through the open door she'd catch a glimpse of the last guests falling off their stools. Or after going to a club near the Ku'damm where musicians from England, the USA or West Berlin would still be sitting at the bar, with faces like young falcons that didn't trust themselves to set off from a safe ledge. Completely immersed in the thin presence of a walled-in metropolis at night and by her own moments, she sweated on the dance floor until she no longer smelt like a hospital. By then it was already day. Outside, when the wind blew in from the east, the streets smelt like coal, and the windows were hung with sheets of darkness as she made her way home on her bike.

What can I bring you?

An elderberry spritzer, she said at last to the waitress for whom the moments that had just passed at that table had not stretched as generously as for her.

Sorry, make that two elderberry spritzers, please, she added softly, my husband's on his way.

Across from the cafe, by the entrance to the cemetery, a bird is now singing its evensong from a tree. A blackbird curses it back. A man at the next table looks over at her, probably because she's just come from the hairdresser's and her blonde hair looks like it would taste like strawberries as soon as you touched it with your lips. An intelligent blonde, her hairdresser likes to say. She looks past the man to the cemetery entrance. Right behind the fence the wind is softly announcing the coming of autumn. Is today one of those days when she will look for one thing and find something else she had missed just as much? She smiles and takes a sip of her spritzer. Even a wrong day can turn out right in the end. Maybe she just had to take her glass and go sit down next to the man, look at his legs beneath the table and say, Do you ever wear white trousers like many men who eventually turn out to have hidden interests? Whatever, in any event, you remind me of someone who once wore white trousers. Don't I remind you of a woman from the past? Have you ever been to Siberia? Or, at the very least, do you ever go to Tegel Airport? I'm over there regularly at weekends. I work in the little room behind the sign for arrivals and departures, there, where the names of cities, flight numbers, gates and times clack upwards from position to position so that you can hear the changes all the way over in the cafe. Believe me, even though the display has long been digital and doesn't make any noise, my colleagues and I still sit over there, in an old room where all the clacking from another time has remained. It's a windowless room, no doors, no ceiling. We eat pumpkin seeds or potato chips and drink tomato juice from the stock of bankrupt airline companies. Yeah, we still update everything by hand, imagine, come on, don't be so lazy, everyone's got to have a little bit of imagination if you want to survive. For you've got to believe me, it's always there, that other world, even if it's invisible in this one.

The man at the neighbouring table sees her, pays. He stands up and leaves. She pulls the business card out of her wallet. Storm | Robert | Schenkendorf . . . As the man crosses the street and makes his way along the cemetery, she compares his gait to that of Robert Storm. A ridiculous undertaking, sure. Storm is far away, in a completely different country, 10,000 kilometres away, and the man over has nothing, I mean nothing of Storm's cheerful ease. On the contrary, with his slightly stooped back and the way he seems to be carrying the weight of the world, he's got more than a little in common with Viktor. She screws up her eyes. No, that's not true either. That guy over there is just a normal guy who's no doubt even more normal in private.

It was raining the day she first spoke to Viktor at Zoo Station. Just a few steps away from the main entrance, a worn old man was pulling out a newspaper dated 13 March 1982 from the trash of a food stand. Viktor was wearing white trousers but wasn't one of those men hanging about the station, hooked on *The Story of Christiane F.* He lived at the edge of the Ruhr district.

That's where I'm from, too, she said.

That's where I was born.

Me too, she went on, so we're both familiar with the same old sad little places where it always rains.

Or they're familiar with us.

At that moment a group of French soldiers was making its way past the old man in the direction of the zebra crossing and ended up pulling him along in their wake. He matched their step, relieved of having a goal until the next corner at least on such a miserable day of begging. That group of foreigners was so much happier than he was, conversing in a language that made you think of music.

At the zebra crossing a white Mercedes stopped to let the soldiers pass.

Between that misty March morning and the March day when Viktor and she broke up many, many years would pass. She saw how he too was watching the scene at the zebra crossing. The glance they exchanged afterwards had something conspiratorial about it. How melancholy that man looked when he wasn't smiling, and how radiant once he finally did. He's probably a good lover, she thought, even though at that point she didn't really have any idea about love. He came, like her, from the country, but had been away from there for some time—or, rather, a long time—already. Paris, Berlin, Bremerhaven, he counted. Now he was living in his old hometown again but had seen the world and brought that tension around his mouth back. Indeed, it looked just like Jeanne Moreau's.

Gedächtniskirche, she said, there, the Kaiser Wilhelm Memorial Church, and pointed to the crumbling spire not even a hundred steps away from the station. Had he asked her to point out all the aspects of the panorama of West Berlin? She'd only been living there a little while herself and had been sternly repeating the word 'Gedächtniskirche' to herself so as not to have to say that, up till then, she hardly had any memories or impressions of the city worth naming. She felt embarrassed and, despite the gloomy weather, put on her sunglasses. She would have preferred curling up like a rabbit under the snow, afraid of being nabbed by a predator. Was this man a predator and she the prey? Was he on the prowl? A good hunter had to be able to put themselves into the animals' position. They also had to know themselves, their own capabilities, weaknesses, instincts.

I know, he said, the stranger who came from the same area she did and maybe even knew the street she'd grown up on.

Sorry?

I'm familiar with the Memorial Church, he repeated, but now in a completely different way.

Oh yeah?

Was he waiting for her to admit that she was turning tricks for drugs, and to pull a letter out of her raincoat as proof, addressed to the social welfare office: I sincerely ask once again for a place in therapy, T-H-E-R-A-P-Y, because every day could cost me my life? Was he waiting for her to ask him to correct any potential mistakes?

How old are you anyway?

Eighteen, and you?

Thirty-six.

What? That old?

Once again, a white Mercedes was stopped at the zebra crossing. Was it the same one? Had it not driven off a long time back? Had it just circled around, looking for a parking space? Or had someone turned back time?

A few minutes later she was putting away her student ID Viktor had used to get them cheaper tickets for the zoo. I want to see the elephants, she said.

Why?

I think they're graceful when they're young.

Then we could come up with a ballet for elephants together, Viktor said.

As they stood in front of the enclosure, one of the animals looked at them with small, clever eyes and shrivelled eyelids, as if it knew something about them, and then pissed in a mighty beam all the way to the edge of the fence. There was something obscene about it. She lit a cigarette and said, I want to get out of here. He grabbed her elbow. It was a touch that tried not to be a touch. Come on, he said, come with me to the polar bears. It sounded like come into my arms.

A moat separated Viktor and her from the animals, whose fur was not actually white, but translucent like his white trousers. I'm going to fall in love with this man, she thought, I'm going to fall in love, though I won't know until the end whether he's the best man in the world or the worst thing that could ever happen to me. He had lifted her out of the nest like a hesitant rabbit.

Ears pointed away from its head, the fur under its chin floppy and baggy like an old woman's, the bear slapped its front paws against each other as if it had heard her thoughts. The second bear climbed on all fours between giant slate-coloured slabs which were irregularly layered into large and even larger plateaus, until it was finally close to his companion. Then the two of them jumped into the moat and swam over to Viktor and her. True mates, Viktor said, and she felt he was referring to her. She noticed how she had begun to tremble, as if he had promised her something beyond his own unattainability. A 'we' that, at the moment, felt like a sad animal.

She turned away, glanced at the trusty piece of Berlin between the zoo and the horizon and wished she were someone else. One that already had a passionate face, with time-rimmed eyes. She wished she'd at least had a hat to cast a shadow across the lines she one day would have when she was twice as old, and everything with her might already have shifted, a few millimetres away from being pretty. She wanted to please this Viktor so badly that she would have sacrificed the shine of her shoulders, the colour of her hair, and even those ten, no, fifteen or eighteen years of life that separated her from him. Because she liked him, a lot in fact, even if he looked like a closed door. She'd fallen in love. There, she said, pointing to a piece of the city on the horizon then immediately lowered her hand. She hardly said a thing after that but hoped her petulant, girlish silence had something secretive about it. Had he chosen her?

He was never supposed to tire of her.

Later she learnt that Viktor was wary and shy, sometimes even timid. Just not when dancing or having sex. He was a delicate man. But others suffered under his fragility more than he did. She only had mascaraed eyelashes, long and hard like a fly's legs. If she'd ever thought she was lonely sometimes until that March day at Zoo Station, she now knew she had never known a truly lonely person until Viktor. He had studied aesthetics and other not-so-important things in Berlin, then in Paris at the Sorbonne, until his residence permit in France was not renewed due to his association with a banned left-wing party. After returning to Germany, Viktor decided to become an architect. A good decision, he later said. The line between right and wrong is sometimes just a question of good or bad luck. For the first time in his life, the decision had given him the feeling that he was on fire not for political views, but for a profession. During his main studies, he worked as an intern for Scharoun at the German Maritime Museum in Bremerhaven and, in the meantime, completed his studies with a thesis full of new, complicated trains of thought that revolved around the theme of perspectives, around systems that were oriented not at vanishing points but within networks and in which old spaces disintegrated. The new spaces were founded in fields of tension that Viktor read for himself like scientific detective stories. Along the way, he half-heartedly designed his practical final project, an alternative highway service area with an adjacent lake that was ideal for swimming in summer and ice skating in winter. Viktor was two years younger than her mother and grew up alone with his own. It was from this being alone that his loneliness must have been born before turning into an older sister. A sister with big, cold breasts whom he loved. No other woman was to seriously interfere.

She glanced at the piece of Berlin between the zoo and the horizon. In ten, fifteen or eighteen years she would no longer be able to say whether on that misty March day the only high-rise on the horizon had been the Haus am Hardenbergplatz or the Hilton to the south instead. For a moment, the silhouette of the city had looked like nothing but slabs of ice, with traces of paws visible at the edges of the fractures as soon as she took a closer look.

Or were they teeth?

Not even two months later she went to go visit Viktor. The train from West Berlin had left in the morning and taken ten hours to reach the edge of the Ruhr. She and Viktor were from neighbouring towns. The buildings at the border between his town and hers were so close together that not even a matchstick would have fit between them.

When Viktor picked her up from the station, the light in the streets slowly changed to something bluish. She found him beautiful, so beautiful that she had trouble concentrating next to him. Did he think she was beautiful, too? Would she cease to give him enough pleasure all too soon? They walked hand in hand through a pedestrian zone where all the stores were just closing; she'd known them for a long time because they had so sadly accompanied her childhood and youth. Whenever they skipped dance class, she'd taken Nina there to McDonald's. But had the area always looked like it had been created after a third war, fought not with bombs but with wrecking balls? When she'd sat with Nina on one of the benches in front of C&A or Peek&Cloppenburg eating liquorice, hadn't she noticed that not only could lose your life in a war but in a pedestrian zone, too? Was it thanks to Viktor that she was no longer the unsuspecting girl on a bench who ate too much liquorice because something completely different was missing?

Viktor taught architecture at a concrete university halfway up a slope, standing forlornly between thin, freshly planted trees and the even thinner wooden supports. Viewed from the city in the valley, the concrete cathedral still teetered sheepishly where a meteorite must have lost it in the early '70s.

Viktor liked it when she wore short skirts and high heels instead of her baggy tracksuit trousers. For his sake she didn't wear a bra. My God, her grandmother thought the first time she heard about Viktor, on the eighth-floor balcony under the satellite dish, that can't be serious. The first time she saw him, she ran her hand through her thinning hair, lit a cigarette and added, He looks like a strawberry ice-cream vendor. Bad, bad, bad. This man is cold and makes your stomach hurt. And do you know how old he'll be when you're in your late thirties? He'll start smelling out of his mouth and ears one day. Yes, he will start to smell. Like an old man. You doing the tango with him yet? I don't want you to come home with a brat and end up like your mother. She used to look like Romy Schneider. Now she just drinks like Romy Schneider.

That's where I live.

Viktor pointed at the broadside of the square to a yellow house with a classically beautiful facade and an ice-cream shop on the first floor. Barberina, she read the neon sign aloud.

Do you know who that is?

No.

That's the gardener's daughter in the opera *The Marriage of Figaro*, she persuades a man to wear women's clothes. Ah, she said, and turned around. At her back, a little smoke from a chimney, happiness on the shiny roofs, two magpies on an antenna. Viktor lived in an old neighbourhood where no bombs had fallen and there weren't any desolate shops. They walked over the paving stones of a church square. They were an Italian yellow and shone in the last evening sun. Bells were ringing. She wished everyone, everyone could see their love at that moment by the way they walked. Seeing them, everyone should remember the tramp Charlie Chaplin and his girl, walking together on the street towards the morning in the last frame of *Modern Times*, until an iris diaphragm engulfs them.

Viktor, she paused, looking at him from the side. There was a strange glow on his face, it was blue. Was it because he was no longer young, but twice her age? Walking to the front door, he ran a hand across his face. The final church bell fell silent. The blue glow on his features, however, remained. That's when a tinge of fear that had been sitting within her since that March day at Zoo Station grew. Was his heart bored? Was it because of her?

Here, he said, and took the key out of his pocket. There were four doorbell plates on the door. Three were unlabelled. Only one had two names written on it in typewriter script, his and a Russian one. Both separated by a space.

She has just paid for the elderberry spritzer at the market-hall cafe, crossed the street and entered Trinity Cemetery. There's a rollator next to the fountain at the entrance, and the sun is low in Berlin Kreuzberg. It has taken on a dark golden hue.

The mistress of the rollator makes a free-handed pilgrimage with a silver milk jug to a light wooden cross. The fresh grave looks as put-together as she does. The August sky is still a deep blue, though the world below is more and more in evening shadow. Busy lilies, boxwoods, fan maples and pink porcelain flowers, noisy plants that like to squat in partial shade are for sale in the market boxes at the nursery behind the entrance. The awning is orange. She drops to her knees and studies the hand-written price tags. I wonder if there are any radish seedlings inside. Being dead also means looking at radishes from below, doesn't it?

Will your vegetables taste like children when you harvest them, dear cemetery gardener of mine? Nina had asked that evening when they'd let themselves be locked in the burial ground at dusk to spend the night. They were eleven or twelve and filled with a quirky love of the life that was waiting for them but had yet to happen. So they fell in love with death for the transitional period instead. They adopted neglected children's graves in the cemetery near the edge of town, where it stank of burning rubbish when the wind was unfavourable. They pulled the weeds, sowed vegetables while the dead children lay still underground. Beans and radishes grew well. Only the tomatoes didn't feel comfortable at first. Tomatoes were nightshades. So, Nina had said, let's stay here today, in the shade of the night. Maybe we'll understand the tomatoes better afterwards.

Become a tomato psychologist, she had replied.

As darkness fell, the foliage in the trees began to speak, speaking more and more clearly of the storm in the offing. Then it rained. They took refuge under the eaves of a nearby toolshed. Ever-thicker fell the curtain of rain as a hooded figure approached across the main path and turned towards the field of children's graves, carrying a plastic bag. Lightning snapped the figure sharply out of the darkness, and the ragged clouds in the sky accompanied them like a herd of extinct animals. Anyone hanging around a graveyard in that weather and at that time could only be dead themselves. She and Nina pressed against each other like rabbits. In front of the bean sticks of a child's grave, the hooded figure squatted down and began to dig. Was this grief, despair, confusion, was this desecration of the grave or vegetable robbery? When the arms had disappeared up to the elbows in the hole in the ground, the figure paused and took out a square packet, curved like a pillow, from the plastic bag. They tossed it into the hole, wiped their eyes, scooped back the earth with their hands, patted it firmly and kicked it once more with their foot. Then, shoulders hunched, disappeared into the rain, which was slowly subsiding. Once only did the figure turn and look over at the toolshed, as if it alone could determine what belonged to the darkness there and what did not. When the rain stopped, she and Nina started to dig in the same place, and Nina said she recognized the face of a rabbit in the frame of the hood. A big, crying rabbit. Reaching into the pillow, which was not a pillow but a constricted, waterproof, brown envelope, Nina was the first to pull her hand back as if burnt. Between crumpled white tissue paper, flat as a furry pancake, was a dead animal with a golden collar.

A rabbit?

No, a mouse, Nina had said. But upon closer inspection, it had turned out to be a rat.


We're about to close, the nursery saleswoman says. She has stepped out in front of the store, cranking the sunshade in over the market crates, on tiptoe.

Cemeteries always close at dusk, you know.

I know.

She looks around. The old woman with the silver milk-jug is still making her pilgrimage between the fountain and the bright cross. I wonder if her husband's in that grave. Her first?

Oh, by the way, my first mouse was a rat! She liked to use that saying in her early animal experiments for her fellow students. How stupid that now only mice are allowed in the lab because they are cheaper and easier to manipulate genetically. Really stupid. At least a rat like that could have broken your heart, letting itself be stroked like a needy man . . .

Have a nice evening, the saleswoman says and goes back inside.

Thank you, she thinks.

Have a nice life, that would've been more fitting.

To the right, the cemetery is bordered not by a wall, but by facades whose windows cast the reflection of a last sun as a pale high beam onto the path in front of her. It is wide and leads straight ahead, with a gentle slope. A path like a magnet that invites its visitors to simply disappear in an overexposed image, until a few steps away a man in white trousers steps out from between two thujas and stops with his back to her.

Viktor's flat on the second floor across from the church was huge, the hallway at least fifteen meters long. A bicycle leant against the radiator between two high doors.

You ride a woman's bike?

Why?

She grabbed the cold radiator and slid into his gaze as if into an embrace.

Can I borrow it?

Yes.

Does it have back pedal brakes?

I don't know.

At one end of the hallway, in the dark, stood a brown piano. The kitchen, at the opposite end, was full of books and unwashed dishes. On the table was a jar of strawberry jam without a lid from a breakfast that hadn't been cleared. Next to it were two used coffee mugs. Viktor poured water into a coffee filter on a porcelain jug. She stood at the window with her back to him to ask: Do you live alone?

The lady at the window blocks my view of the landscape, he answered after a while. She did not understand what he meant, and he went on making coffee.

Viktor slept in a storeroom next to the study, on the narrow door he had unhinged from between the two rooms, a makeshift bed. The foam mattress on the door was thin as sandwich spread when she lay down. Asceticism—was this his arrangement against any kind of nicer living? He would not be able to answer her question for the next fifteen years they were together. She hadn't had much practice with men. Still, she wasn't afraid of lurching from one sensation to the next with Viktor. She was only afraid of the door. She didn't want to fall asleep there. She thought, The surface we're lying on isn't a bed, but a trap door, and it goes on, four stories deep, then floor, then heat, glow, red, abyss—death.

Night followed, turned into morning, which they turned back into night until night fell again, losing and finding each other over and over. Whether what they were doing had anything to do with love, she could not have said. Viktor, she might have asked more than once, One day, will you love me from your soul? She let it pass. Because she herself was still inexperienced and clumsy, she did not immediately notice his somewhat solemn, almost metallic way of making love. Later on, she did. Even when it lasted longer, they hardly grew any closer. *Come*, he said, but always made her come alone. He always paid attention right before climax, saying, Scream! Scream! Then left her empty and alone.

A few nights later, Viktor, elbow in the thin foam mattress and head in one hand, talked about the past. But they were very different stories from the ones her grandmother told out on the balcony under the satellite dish. He'd been together with most women, yes, even with his wife, from whom he lived separately, Viktor said, for political and erotic reasons, which for him were almost the same thing.

Ah, she said, and lay still. She didn't want more detail.

In 1964, he said, when I was a little older than you are now, things changed once. That had nothing to do with politics. I danced in a pavilion on the Ostende promenade with a saleswoman from a Brussels department store. Three years later, the department store burnt down. Hundreds of people died in the fire. On the second floor, in the children's clothing department, a young employee had been the first to discover the flames, according to the press. You, he went on, must've been three at the time.

Was the young employee the girl from Ostende? she whispered into the darkness of the storeroom.

Maybe, possibly.

Did she manage to get to safety too?

Probably.

Would you have liked to see her again?

Perhaps, yes, he said, but now that I'm twice her age, I've found another eighteen-year-old who feels just like her.

Who?

You.

Me?

Probably, Viktor said, yes, perhaps.

The feeling of being mistaken for a memory and nevertheless not meant at all in the end remained even over the years to come. She would call the feeling 'OSTENDE'. Yes, it remained, was worse than jealousy. It didn't burn, it seeped. It didn't make her particularly angry but addicted. Yes, this feeling made her dependent and at the same time gave her a surprisingly sharper contour. Nina's contour, she had sometimes thought later. That night, towards morning, on that door with the foam mattress she'd straddled him, her right hand braced against a shelf, and two fingers of her left in Viktor's mouth. She had given the orders, for the first time, and had enjoyed a second feeling that sat on top of Ostende. She had enjoyed the more bitter struggle, a struggle which would bind her for a long time to this man who knew so much more than she did. Whose currency in companionship was words, but who took on something nervous, uncertain when he kissed her. There was something seductive in the contrast between Viktor with clothes and Viktor without. He also wanted to be casual naked but didn't succeed, and she thought, It's because of me, only me! With me, one day, he'll be completely unfaithful to himself in the dark. The contrast between Viktor's outward agility and the way his face dissolved when they embraced told of a secret. That kind of tension, not knowing yet wanting to know, remained until the end of their relationship, kept them bound to each other even when it was over but simply limping on.

That night, when Ostende had first appeared, she had seen Viktor lying beneath her with her eyes closed. Behind her lids, he had been wearing women's clothes. More precisely, a petticoat, it was old and purple.

As morning crept in, she lay beside him, among the shelves of dusty old newspapers that grew in piles up the wall of his storeroom, longing to be archives. From time to time a breeze brushed over her from the open window. It was early May. The bird-clock outside announced it was just about five. They both lay there listening, staring at the ceiling: two fish on a white platter, two salmon on a sideboard, waiting for guests at a wedding that would never happen. She would not have been able to say how the image came into her head. Had she seen it somewhere, read it? Viktor pointed to the high ceiling painted with flowers and arranged in the colours of a happy time. Look, there at the edge, where ceiling and wall meet, there, at dawn, like now, there's a narrow purple line that disappears as soon as it really gets light.

In the morning when she woke up Viktor was gone. Wrapped in a bath towel, she walked down the hall, opening all the doors. The rooms facing the inner courtyard were in shadow. They were the colour of emptiness and rain. Those facing the street, the smell of something stale.

Here's the key to the flat, Viktor had said, I won't be back till evening.

From the kitchen she heard the ticking of a clock, from the bathroom the clacking of the gas boiler. At the far end of the hallway, where a brown piano stood, two doors met at a shallow angle. The left one led to a storage closet, full of labelled boxes full of books and old paint buckets. Between them was an old deckchair with a bare red down-blanket on it, next to it orphaned flowerpots and a toolbox. She opened the door on the right and thought, What kind of place have I stumbled into? The room was obviously furnished for guests and laid out with a light-coloured carpet, its wool upright like unmown grass. Then she saw the roll-top cabinet. In front of it a wire coat hanger. While bending it into a hook, she had decided to never get married.

The windows of the facade to the right of Trinity Cemetery still cast reflections of sun across the evening path. But it has lost some of its magic since this man stepped backwards onto it through some thujas. Aloud, he recites: For, nearing death, one doesn't see death; but stares / beyond, perhaps with an animal's vast gaze. / Lovers, if the beloved were not there / blocking the view, are close to it, and marvel . . . Now the man hesitates but does not turn around. He clears his throat and continues: Yes, lovers . . . are close to it and marvel . . . / As if by some mistake, it opens for them / behind each other . . . But neither can move past / the other . . .

Having finished his lines, he raises a grey file over his head: 'The Eighth Duino Elegy' by Rilke, he says. The listeners throng closer around him, carrying colourful backpacks they are too old for, and thin two-tone weather jackets although it is August and there is no rain in sight. The man, however, is wearing white trousers. Rilke, he repeats, flipping through his folder as if to count the pages. He still has his back towards her. His hair is rather long and not that neat. A friendly listener from the group smiles at her. Come on over, her lips say soundlessly. For a moment the man is distracted but does not turn around to see who among his circle is speaking in the language of fish. He slams the folder shut and recites by heart: And we: spectators, always, everywhere, / turned toward the world of objects, never outward. / It fills us. We arrange it. It breaks down. / We rearrange it, then break down ourselves . . .

The man runs a hand through his hair.

Am I boring you? he asks his listeners.

No answer.

What do you think, are the dead bored here, too?

No answer.

Are the dead perhaps always bored?

Not always, forever, she answers, unasked, at his back.

Finally the man turns around. As the friendly listener circles the group and walks towards them, a dreamlike white reflection passes over the man's face like the sweep of a spotlight. Someone in the buildings above the cemetery wall has probably opened or shut a window, casting a last echo of sun.

What a day.

She recognizes that face.

Or does she only recognize the white trousers?

Tours take place regularly, every Monday and Friday. They cost eight euros. Only on All Saints' Day and Halloween is it two euros more expensive. Here you are.

The friendly listener is now standing in front of her and presses a piece of paper into her hand.

'When Time Becomes Eternity' is written above the portrait of a pensive stone angel.

Schenkendorfstraße then, a few minutes away from Trinity Cemetery, has nothing exciting about it, with the exception of the fact that Robert Storm lives there. She has been standing for a few minutes in front of No. 7, a renovated house with French balcony lattices in lime green, and a lime-green front door. No one appears. 'Stein / Storm' is on the doorbell plate for the second-floor front building. No hyphen, just a slash between the names.

How had she and Johann been together on that doorbell plate? Neither connected nor with a slash, but simply separated by a space.

## 29.1

Drive to see a friend who's just broken up with her partner. On the outskirts of town, little end row-house and the corpse of a forgotten Christmas tree at the bus stop. At dinner she only talks about herself, then him. I've known her for a long time. She has always liked animals. On the dog sofa next to her designer couch, which he left behind, an old dog, awake but sickly. A street dog from Mallorca who constantly jumps up for no reason, although he can no longer jump, to yap at enemies who aren't there. Sometimes he just falls on his side, the mutt. Epilepsy, my friend says. Her black cardigan is full of dog hair.

Today, sun between the buildings, but only briefly. Today, the question to all the dead I know: Are you all still there, where you are now?

## 19.2

Irmgard is buried at five below zero in a cemetery in the middle of the allotment garden settlement south of Teltow Canal. Right next door to the Berlin rubbish collection's transfer station. Irmi has been given a burial by the social welfare office and will lie diagonally opposite Marianne Rosenberg's father. There must have been five hundred mourners at his funeral. There are five of us and only one is really sad. Ilya. In my Volvo Man's borrowed Volvo we raced over the A100 in the direction of Dresden. Ilya up front, with his mother at the wheel, two acquaintances of Irmi's and me in the back because I don't have a driver's license. Ilya's mother told us about Irmi's flat, but instead of flat she says, Egyptian burial chamber. The stain on the floorboards where Irmi died, on two unfolded moving boxes, is still visible, she says, and under the bed she found three pruning shears, eight garden shears, various plant fertilizers and a small axe, plus twenty kilos of shrink-wrapped sheep's cheese and five hundred packets of baking soda. The pantry was cleaned out yesterday by two guys from Chechnya and a Pole with vans. Maybe Irmi was possessed by a ghost who once starved to death, wonders one acquaintance in the back seat. Let's hope the ghost was burnt in the crematorium with her, says the other.

We arrive half an hour early, and eat rolls with onions at the snack stand across from the cemetery. An early funeral feast, says Ilya. Later, as we walk behind the funeral director and a sealed dark vase containing Irmi's ashes, we smell like a snack stand. *I'm like you*, Ilya sings softly as we pass Rosenberg's grave. The funeral director carries Irmi's remains before him like those of a queen. Her final resting place is right next to the fence facing the motorway. One acquaintance throws the mouse book into the open grave, which Irmi had always loved to read, and Ilya's mother a cross against vampires. I only have flowers with me, because I didn't know Irmi that well, and the other acquaintance has a wish, which she says loudly into the cold air: Hopefully you'll make more friends where you are now. Ilya says, I can only agree with that. He wears a black coat with bare spots along the button strip and cuffs, which is too thin for the weather. I wonder if his mother actually called him Ilya because of Ilya Richter. Back in the borrowed Volvo from my Volvo driver, Ilya's mother passes around a photo. A blonde, very pretty girl is lying on a sofa in an old-fashioned pink blouse—one you could find labelled 'vintage' now at a charity shop—and has a baby on her belly. That is Irmi, smiling, and the baby stretches its little fists like antennae to the sky. Irmi lost her brother at seventeen, then her mother, both in the same year, but stayed on living alone in two rooms in Neukölln.

Everything, everything comes from the past . . .

Later in the afternoon one of the two acquaintances will go back to Irmi's flat and pick up thirty little teddy bears for her workshop with the mentally ill.

**13.3**

Into this room, right into my frontal lobe, where a red light's always blinking in the same corner and warms me, regardless of whether I remember happier days or imagine moments of a more successful life, one day I am going to write an autobiography in this room, this room that's always been the same, an autobiography in which I leave out the most important thing.

Me.

And the Volvo.

# TUESDAY

Look closely, the roses aren't roses. Not painted ones, anyway. You can't tell if you don't know, can you?

One by one, the boss turns three framed pictures around that have been leaning against the cold office radiators ever since everything was renovated. The petals, the boss says, with a barely noticeable American accent, are made of duck tongues, the rest of deer eyelashes and, in some places, fish eyes. The artist grew up next to her parents' fattening farm, where the animals simultaneously ate one another's tails. There, as a girl, she cut up slaughtered pigs and put them in bags. As an adult, she went back to the slaughterhouse of her childhood one day after her husband left her after twenty years of marriage. She obtained meat scraps and offal and reconstructed her husband's face from it, then fed it to a starving dog. After a few hours, however, the carcass face began to smell so disgusting that she threw it in the garbage . . .

Well, everything, everything comes from the past, from when you were a child, the boss says, fanning herself with both hands and throwing her head back. It looks childlike. The boss doesn't have kids, but she does have discipline, ambition, grace, a special sense of art and moments of disarming innocence that no one in this neurobiology institute has ever been able to get used to.

She was born in Dallas.

It is Tuesday morning. For almost ten years now, she has been working in the small cubicle next to the large office of her boss, who at the time was looking for an additional project manager for the lab with some administrative duties. This turned into the job of a secretary and a girl friday of sorts. Nevertheless, the boss likes to say to guests that this secretary has a PhD, and points to her with the hands of a conductor, as if to draw attention to an orchestra's soloist. But she always looks impassively past the theatrical gesture and towards the espresso cups that are next to the tin for pepper chocolates on a small roll-top cabinet by the door. What do the brown cups in a cosy circle remind her of? Of siblings who don't exist in her life or the children she doesn't have? Of Johann? And because of its colour, a chestnut tree? Or only of its leaves with brownish edges that say the days are getting shorter again?

Or do the cups in a cosy circle remind her of the weekly circle of a support group back on the Rhine, which she left behind for the job offer which came soon after she'd left Johann?

For some people even a circle of chairs can be a home.

Everything, everything comes from the past, from when you were a child, the boss says again, running her hand over one of the picture frames. Yes, everything, everything that is painful down through the core of your being, reappears. With me as a character defect or, as here on the rose pictures, as art. All animal carcasses, she says, but what a power of colour, what grace and ultimately what proof that ventures like this one, indeed that modern art in general demands more of our cognitive areas than a Rembrandt.

What a woman. More whirr than woman, she thinks, nods to the boss, better comprehending a racing bike than Rembrandt.

Are you still listening to me?

She nods again.

By the way, the boss continues, I couldn't care less if someone gets upset about a few dead animals. Or do you find the pictures disgusting?

I always find dead animals disgusting.

Our mice, too?

Yes.

Is that a fact? I got used to dead animals long ago in my life, yes, I got used to quite a few other things, for example, the fact that at a certain point in my career, men were no longer passionately interested in me as a lover but only as an animal-rights activist.

This, the building supervisor of the new Düsseldorf flat had told her and Johann, this was a real Egyptian burial chamber. The woman didn't die in bed, but on a piece of cardboard. Right here! Like an animal!

His breath smelt of onions. He drew the outline of South America on the laminate in the darkest room with his foot. She was an overweight, lonely old bitty. Hopefully, she'd have more of a connection where she was now than she did here . . .

How old was the lady at the time? she asked, leaning her head against the doorframe.

Fifty-four.

Oh, man . . .

She turned to the balcony and looked at a small tree in a plastic pot that someone must have forgotten. Next to it, in the empty space of a stool, a bunch of noisy little birds had gathered. Briefly. Then they were gone again.

She went back into the room, stood next to Johann and slipped a hand into the back pocket of his jeans. Soon it would be New Year's Eve again, the fourth of nine they would spend together till the end of their story. Six weeks earlier they'd been asked to leave the previous flat above the cabaret which Johann had so patiently refurbished. The building had been renovated and sold off, one floor at a time.

Fifty-four, she repeated, they say you grow strange with age.

She didn't become strange, she was always like that, the building supervisor said. Now that she's dead, burnt and buried, feel free to look around. The place isn't haunted. It's just been empty for too long, but it was fully occupied, I tell you, always just full, full, full. We removed twenty kilos of shrink-wrapped sheep's cheese and hundreds of packages of baking powder, among other things, from the previous tenant, to say nothing of the garden tools and teddy bears. Suddenly she thought of Viktor. One day he'd told her that he had photographed the room in which his mother had died with a self-made pinhole camera as soon as the dead woman was carried out. Would you be able to tell if someone had just died in that room? he had wanted to know. Had death laid itself as invisible writing on the things, in order to rest there briefly? Viktor's camera was made of a cardboard box. In the back he slid in photographic paper. The aluminium foil in front of it he crushed with a needle, but only a little. Done. In the five pictures he took that way there were white shadows and ghosts because of the long exposure times. What comprises such a moment? Viktor had asked her at the time. That something still remains when someone leaves, and can be seen by anyone who isn't blind, right? Back then, because of the pictures, the sight of which had always made him smile, he'd even forgotten to cry, Viktor recalled.

Fifty-four is too early to die and not really old at all, she said to the building supervisor.

Not really, he replied.

She would have liked to ask where the poor bitty's things from the Egyptian burial chamber had gone, aware of her own mortality while also afraid of one day becoming neglected herself. But she went out onto the balcony. The supervisor followed. He briefly stroked the doorframe with his right hand, exactly where she had just rested her head.

Then the three of them stood on the balcony and looked over the parapet. Three storeys down in the courtyard, the stump of a tree that had been cut down stuck out of the paving. A copper beech, the supervisor said. Even survived the war, but not the Danish investors from the retirement home across the way. But here there's already a replacement.

He tapped the tip of his shoe against the plastic pot. The little tree must have seeded itself. A sweet chestnut, the supervisor said. In five years it'll be three times as tall and cast a small shadow in the evening, if you're still living here. By the way, here are the keys . . .

He jingled a bunch as if wanting to play with a child or a cat. She was the first to grab it. He then looked at Johann. It's not attractive, the flat, he said, but it's cheap, and centrally located. You can do all your shopping on foot, go to the movies and the Wehrhahn S-Bahn stop right outside the entrance makes for a quick escape.

Johann laughed. For no reason, she thought.

Escape from the city, I mean, the supervisor said stoically.

In the afternoon she and Johann had played foosball in the canteen of the Schauspielhaus between three and five, when it was deserted and the food counter was closed with a silver roller blind. Johann had behaved as if he still belonged to the life of the theatre in those dead hours, even though he had long since stopped working at any theatre at all. If you want to be happy for an hour, sleep, a Chinese proverb proclaimed. If you want to be happy for a day, go fishing. If you want to be happy for a year, have a fortune. If you want to be happy for a lifetime, love your work.

Johann was out of work.

Fuck, he said after losing the third game in a row.

Yeah, yeah, poor guy, she replied.

When had he actually begun saying *fuck* so often, and for no apparent reason? Was life itself fucked? She looked at Johann across the table. Last Saturday he'd ridden his racing bike to the cheap barbershop in the industrial park and returned looking like an inmate with a machine-shorn scalp. There had been something rushed, time-worn about him ever since. Once he had seemed tall, handsome and capable to her. Once she had felt that he could protect her, this man had seemed so different to her on that New Year's Eve. How had he actually got past her mind's snap judgements that night? Did he have the right password? Or did she when she'd said, Kiss me, you don't love your girlfriend any more anyway? Oh Johann, she thought, if we were at least still arguing outside the cinema about the right movie or at Ikea about the grain of a closet door. If only milk would spill out of your grubby burlap bag on the last day of the year. It had never been about anything fundamental between them until now, which didn't mean they weren't doing something fundamentally wrong.

Fuck, Johann repeated. His face had something sheepishly sinister, despondent, but also somewhat opinionated.

What's so *fucked*, Johann?

We are, for being in such a precarious position, Beautiful.

Don't take it personally, she replied, and tossed in the next ball.

They were both almost forty. No one had told them that the second half of life would be so much harder than the first. But yeah, fucked, that's what it was. There just wasn't enough room for lucky winners, but plenty of room for losers like them, people without the right invitations to the important receptions. Only once, in the slipstream of her doctoral advisor, had she been invited to a major social event as part of a summer academy, and Johann two or three times to conferences as a representative of his artistic director who had no taste for ambitious colleagues. They had both smelt of sweat on those occasions, even though they'd showered, and had had a whole province at their heels on the gleaming parquet floor as they crossed the room shoulder to shoulder to get to the buffet. She'd even had to leave one of those evenings early with a drunken latchkey child by the name of Johann on her hand.

Are we stupid?

No.

Yes, we are.

No.

Yes, repeated Johann, and scored a goal.

Fuck, he said in glee. That's what finally being a winner again felt like.

And I'll tell you another thing, Beautiful . . .

Johann had run his hands along the table's wooden frame.

. . . from now on, it's not what they've made us that counts, but what we make of what they've made us.

He won the next three games in a row.

Three oblong rooms, a tiny bathroom with a chipped ceramic tub and a windowless kitchen where they could put the red-lacquered wall cabinet. She had chosen the nicer room for herself right on the evening the keys were handed over, with a view of the S-Bahn. The first one came at 4.30 in the morning and the last one long after midnight. If she couldn't sleep, she could abandon herself to the tenderness of passing trains or watch the early risers on the platform from the window. At the moment, however, everything had disappeared behind a bunch of chestnut trees. Johann's room faced the back, at the other end of the flat, but had the balcony. Without insulation, it would be too cold there in winter and unbearably hot in summer. The view out his window was of the nursing home, with a glass dome on top, beneath which the nuns who worked as caregivers there prayed five times a day. He put his racing bike on the balcony and decided to put the bed they shared in their room. In his, he built a huge new desk with two phone lines, a scanner and a large computer screen, which is where he would manage his feelings of helplessness. If she was in bad a mood, she would wash her hair or open the window, no matter what the temperature. She told herself that every kind of weather was fine and that one day good news would arrive.

Or a dear visitor.

A pale, full moon wandered millimetre by millimetre along the gap between the rooftops of the buildings across the street as they stood barefoot and leaning against each other on the balcony one night. Inside, a *Tatort* rerun was on. Johann lit a cigarette. The wind blew the smoke into her face. Barely perceptible, there was a sudden fear, a languor. They were sad, but carried on cheerfully, attempting a kiss as if nothing was wrong, and then looking at each other and not knowing what to do. In a window opposite, the light went out. She disengaged herself from his shoulder and tiredly played with the leaves of the sweet chestnut with her bare toes.

You could go gay, Johann.

What a suggestion, what would happen to us?

At least you'd have your boys' network.

Fuck, I'm too old for that, Beautiful.

For what, exactly?

For both . . .

She began to cry. And he remained standing. From the balcony one could wave to the nuns. It was past eleven already, Johann said, time for a beer somewhere.

No, no one was practicing piano next door.


After his unemployment benefits ran out the following year Johann started cleaning houses and did gardening for two euros more an hour too. She continued to slide from one editing job to another. Sometimes, when she needed to get a bit of fresh air between analyses of test persons, correcting commas and theories on mirror neurons and empathy (which sometimes worked themselves up into the novelistic), she would accompany Johann to his job or wait for him afterwards. One Saturday, while on the way to pick him up from the poshest part of town, a man stood on the pavement in front of the house, blocking Johann's view. Trimmed boxwood-hedge tops lay scattered about the two of them. She had braked. Her bike squealed. At the familiar sound, Johann jerked his head up and looked at her over the man's shoulder. The sleeves of his blue plaid shirt were rolled up to his elbows. She saw the strong hairy forearms which had once led her to assume Johann knew exactly what that meant between a man and a woman. He turned off the electric hedge trimmer. Soft music came from an open window, something Spanish, but nothing you could stomp your heels to. The man standing in front of Johann shoved his hands into his pockets and sauntered over to a bike, one of those fancy red ones with tires as narrow and bright as ginger snaps. As he passed, he greeted them without taking his hands out of his pockets. Then he looked at Johann and unlocked the bike. As he rode along the pavement close to them both, he slapped Johann's shoulder. There was something obscene about it. He must have meant the butt. Johann smiled confidingly. When the bike disappeared around the corner, Johann and she stood alone, the two of them, on the quiet street for rich people until a fat Airbus approaching the airport roared overhead. She said, It serves them right, having planes pull at the tops of their heads and spraying jet fuel onto their thinning hair. Johann shrugged his shoulders, acknowledging her social envy, and began to pick up the cut hedge branches.

She had bent down to help him, the traitor.

When they got home, she saw that the chestnut leaves outside her window facing the S-Bahn—where she'd been standing more and more often and for longer and longer periods of time—already bore an autumnal brown edge. How long had they been living here? One year? Two? Three? What was she waiting for? Theatre itself is pure waiting, Johann had said just the other day. Drama means waiting for something to happen, for the villains to be punished, for the lovers to find each other, for the messenger to finally arrive. Beckett's innovation, Johann said, was that he refused to let it happen. Waiting became pure process, and do you know, Beautiful, in which play?

*Waiting for Godot?* she'd asked cautiously.

Exactly, Johann had said, and now something else. Theatre and Christian dramaturgy have a lot in common. Always gathering at the same time to wait. Showing up at the same hour, in the same place, means being saved.

Yes, that's right, she'd said even more quietly and almost in love again right there at their shared kitchen table, pushing the pot of spaghetti bolognese back and forth a few centimetres. Right! Johann hadn't talked that much in a long time. And, since he no longer worked at the theatre, what had actually encouraged her to judge that he might be friendlier and more approachable than Viktor, if nowhere near as intelligent? That he was the type of man who always liked to take out his mobile to show pictures of racing bikes he'd like to have with a meagre, though permanent, smile?

Who had actually committed treason here?

On another Saturday after Johann had once again cleaned *the rich people's house*, as she called it, they rode to the bench by the ferry landing, the one Johann called *our bench*, but she referred to as the Bench of Silence.

In his saddlebag the beer bottles rattled against each other.

On the Rhine towards Holland, a barge hung low in the water at the same height next to them. On deck there was a man, a woman, a small, red, rather battered car and above them laundry hanging out to dry. Johann had put his left hand on her saddle and was pushing her up the dyke as they rode. We can have his house rent-free for half a year, he said on the bike close behind her. He's going abroad on business, maybe even staying longer—he's met a woman.

She turned as she lifted herself out of the saddle and pedalled harder.

Is she pregnant?

No, Chinese.

Johann smiled. Fox-like somehow, she thought. Looking at his lips, she became aware of her own.

Is she young?

The Chinese girl? Mid-thirties, I think, some kind of leftover woman.

Leftover woman, what's that supposed to mean—thank you very much?

That's what they call everyone in China who has a good education and good income but no husband, because no Chinese man wants a partner more qualified than he is.

Who says so?

He does.

And now this leftover woman wants to marry the man you clean for?

Why not? He's German and unafraid of smart women.

You sure know a lot about him, your fancy employer. You seem to have spoken intimately, she said, looking ahead again and pedalling even harder.

Things were changing. It wasn't always clear how, but it always happened without those involved noticing or wanting to notice right away. When did she stop seeing them together, when did she close her eyes? She had imagined the end of their relationship more than once: in one version, Johann bumped into the nearest woman at the pasta shelf in the supermarket who implored him, Kiss me, you don't love your girlfriend any more anyway. In another, some woman from the past came back, not necessarily named Nina. Visions of separation, she knew, liked to pretend that they were already memories of something that imposed itself as a real event without having really happened. Remembering and experiencing were almost the same thing from the brain's point of view, she knew. So was pure imagination. Why else had she studied neurobiology for so long? Remembering and experiencing were close together in her grey drawers, sometimes without a clear partition. But what good was this knowledge to her? She stood on the side helplessly, while her love slowly ran out of air like an old balloon. Another woman had probably long been better for Johann than she was, she thought.

She didn't have to be Chinese.

Johann let go of her saddle. On the barge the woman sat down on deck behind the wheel of a small red car to touch-up her lips in the rear-view mirror.

Did you bring hand cream? Johann asked, overtaking her, his hands off the handlebars.

As the distance between them increased and she could no longer hear the beer bottles rattling, he took off his long-sleeved T-shirt while driving and tied it around his hips. There was something calm and serene about that, something carefree and acrobatic, and she liked it. In fact, she liked it a lot.

A Rhine ferry docked a few steps from their bench. It sailed every quarter of an hour. Four passengers got off at the landing and walked close to the Bench of Silence. The two women in front walked away, the two men followed. Johann's beer bottle was already empty.

Oh him, he may not be much better than the others, said one woman, but I wonder if this Obama will become president soon? I don't think so, said the other, but he looks good. She pushed her sunglasses into her hair, as if Obama had glanced at her directly from America. The men talked about the Chinese being dangerous in themselves because they worked all the time for little money. Well, Johann said, rolling his beer bottle between his palms and watching the two couples turn off toward the dyke. The one with the gold barrette in her yellow-grey braid belongs to the man in the dark-blue baseball cap, and comes from Saxony, where, as the old saying has it, the most beautiful women in Germany live. But there are exceptions everywhere. The one with the sunglasses in her hair belongs to the man in the NYPD cap. He's a real estate agent or a horse stable owner or both, and all four of them smoked in bed when they were young.

So did we, she said. Johann laughed.

When had it started to feel like it was over between them and just limping on? She already knew that feeling.

What was it like with you and Viktor? Johann asked, right then.

I've told you.

I don't mean the relationship, I mean the end.

Now she laughed but looked aside so that he wouldn't see how serious she was.

Hey, Beautiful, what is it?

Johann gently nudged her foot with his own.

What was that feeling when Viktor and you broke up?

An Ostende feeling, she would have liked to reply, but said instead, Oh feelings, feelings, what can I say?

You were just thinking about him, weren't you?

You can read minds?

I can see when you're thinking about him, you bite your cuticles and look forlorn.

You think you're pretty smart . . .

I think you were quite lonely together with this Viktor.

She looked at him. Johann. Almost any woman would envy him. Not because of his big hands, with which he could lay electrical cable but because of a silent promise that was at the core of his being. Standing at the window next to Johann a woman could let the sky above the building across the street move along at the slow speed of the earth, through both the fat and the lean years.

In a moment of affection, she pressed hard on his knee.

What are you doing? he asked.

Immobilizer, she said.


Shortly after bells had rung in the evening, the ferry docked for the last time on that side of the river. Colourful fairy lights flickered in the beer gardens across the water. Laughter came in shreds over the river and Johann wrote the names of possible invitees for his next birthday on his forearm with a biro. The party was to be in June. The list wasn't particularly long. Old friends from Singen were there, but hardly anyone from the theatre. Life was short, but some days felt like for ever.

Finally, the helmsman and the cashier got off the last ferry of the day and walked separately to their small cars parked on the dyke, a few steps behind the bank. Johann said nothing. She waited. Because sometimes he could be lured out of silence with silence.

Not today.

As they cycled back, the bottles in Johann's bike bag clinking against each other empty, louder with every bump in the path. Dusk sharpened the lights along the dyke. The sounds of engines came from a row of garages to their right, running parallel with the sloshing of waves lapping against the Rhine bank to their left. Johann braced his hand against her saddle again, even though they were on a slope.

We just have to look after the house, he said to her ear, look after the garden, water it, rake up the leaves in autumn. We have to pay heating and water, otherwise we live for free in the best part of town.

In the best part of town, she said, listen to how that sounds. To be honest, I wouldn't even want to hang over the fence there if I was dead.

Where they turned away from the river and towards the city, she saw, as always, a row of empty barns by the side of the road, harvests long gone. Why didn't they use them any more?

I want to stay where we are, at Wehrhahn, she said, I don't want to be unfaithful to where I live.

Do you realize how that sounds?

How does it sound?

Like unfaithful to whom you're with, said Johann.


Later, once it was Sunday already and she was at the kitchen sink trying to clean the groove in-between the sink and the worktop with vinegar and a sponge, Johann hugged her from behind. Finished reading Sebald, he declared, ate a jam sandwich while reading and got back my courage. He placed a handleless red mug down next to the sink. 'Hero of Labour' inscribed on a red background. Viktor had found it along with other refuse from the GDR at the beginning of the '90s and taken it out of love for things that no one wanted any more. Viktor had disappeared from her life, but the cup was still there and sometimes spoke to her in that special way Viktor had taught her to listen to. Johann grabbed some milk from the fridge, took a sip, put it down next to the sink, and announced, I'm going for a jog along the S-Bahn tracks. It was already night outside, a terribly wet and gusty March night, the kind that tore at the clouds that were already in a hurry. He slammed the door behind him harder than a gust of wind. The carton of milk toppled. She watched it trickle down the sideboard.

Hey, she said, hey, what's all this about? What are you trying to tell me?

That's what it used to be like, remember? the dripping milk replied.

And there she'd remained, right next to the spilt milk, undecided whether to yawn, cry in the bathroom or water the chestnut tree on the balcony.

Tuesday lunchtime, shortly after one. Raoul is standing in the doorway to her office. Instead of asking how she's doing, he recites the canteen menu. Meanwhile, she turns the boss' rose pictures over so that they are leaning face forward against the cold office radiators again. Not roses, she thinks, just animal remains, no petals. Duck tongues. And Raoul says, There's also lamb stew, and eggs in mustard sauce and something else I immediately forgot because I don't like it. She notices something on the tip of her tongue. Just as she fished the stubby hair out of her mouth with her thumb and forefinger, she thought, Not mine! That's a deer's eyelash.

On the way to the canteen Raoul tells her about a dinner invitation he'd had that past Friday. That Friday, she thinks, was the last Friday night in my life when a certain Robert Storm and someone like me were still strangers.

Shabbat on the second floor, upstairs, Raoul says, that was quite new to me.

Would be new for me too, she thinks.

The new neighbour is a rabbi who'd come from New York with his family. Now he teaches as a visiting professor at the Institute for Jewish Studies at the University of Potsdam. A figure-skating princess was there, too, all in white, but she introduced herself as a manager from Jerusalem, and then a rabbi my age arrived, who wanted to take off his kipa during the aperitif, which the older rabbi laughingly forbade. Have you ever been to something like that? Raoul asks, calling the lift.

Are you familiar with it, the breaking of bread and singing and all?

No.

Me neither, says Raoul, but then we talked. Yes, there's general anxiety about the future, but no, something like Auschwitz, that will never happen again, we all said at the table. The 45th, who's now president, the figure-skater said, his family's from Germany, right? Yeah, a *meister* from Germany, the younger rabbi replied in German. But other than that, we only spoke in English.

The lift arrives. The door opens with a ping.

And then, Raoul says, as the door closes again and the two of them ride down, then it occurred to me that this 45th president was born the same year as both Bush and Clinton. All three were born in 1946! I said that right away too. All three, I said, were born in the year one after the Second World War.

She looks into the tinted cabin mirror.

A year later than Viktor, she thinks.

Bush paints, Raoul says.

What does he paint? Flowers? Since he had such a sad childhood? she snaps, unwittingly.

No, portraits of Afghan soldiers playing golf with one leg missing, Raoul, laughs.

He probably does self-portraits, in the nude, but with two legs.

Ping. The lift door opens to the ground floor.

Why does it smell like fish in here? she asks as the door closes with a soft smacking sound behind her.

Fish, exactly, Raoul says, earlier I'd forgotten about the fish.

At the table by the window overlooking the Institute courtyard, there are two people less than the Twelve Apostles and they are talking about upcoming weekend, although it is only Tuesday, but a beautiful one, one with a last August blue and a light silver haze. The air has been cooler than over the last few weeks. When she looks out of her office window in the morning, there is a meditative spaciousness above the bicycle racks five floors below, where the first yellow leaves are falling from the trees. Chestnut time, or time of change?

Is Viktor still alive? What's Johann up to?

Saturday, Alasdair says, I'll be mountain biking in the woods alone. It reminds me of being back home in Glasgow. Sofia says this weekend her new boyfriend wants to introduce her to his family. Tim wants to go to a reading by a novelist who knows a lot about astrophysics and nevertheless writes exciting books. Maria will cook Chinese at Radu's and the-handsome-Raoul's place, with whom she had a brief affair last summer. Theres will argue with her boyfriend in the little end rowhouse about wind turbines and nuclear power, as usual. Paola has to study German, while Mike will stay at home and laze on his sofa, slather on the new ointment for neurodermatitis and watch *Total Recall* for the umpteenth time, he says. Read Oliver Sacks instead, Tim says, he's amazing. Daniel munches on a roll and remains silent. A young woman from the bar staff very slowly cleans the vacant table next to them with a shabby yellow rag and listens on. When Alasdair from Glasgow, Sofia from Corinth, Tim from Darmstadt, Maria from Barcelona, Radu from Romania, Paola from Turin, Mike from Rostock walk behind Theres Grau from Graubünden and return their dishes, Raoul from Cuba remains sitting at the table near her.

And you, what are you doing next weekend?

She shrugs and looks at the half-eaten roll which Daniel has left behind.

A secret? Are you involved with someone? A boyfriend?

Raoul gazes at her with those dark eyes that are not-so-special in his country. Here they are. If she were to look at him for too long, her heart would flutter and nothing would make sense any longer.

Anyway, he says, I'm coming in to the institute this weekend. I often do. I sit down alone in front of my microscope for a few hours and have my peace. When it gets boring, I stand by the window for a bit. Do you know how deserted the institute grounds are then?

I do.

She hunches her shoulders, the way she sometimes would while dancing with couples when she can't master the steps.

I'm thirty-six, Raoul says, if it doesn't work out with the team leadership here in the lab, well . . .

Thirty-six, she repeats, ah . . .

Johann had also been thirty-six when they'd met on New Year's Eve, and his bed was no wider than the door to the bathroom. Instead of studying, he'd made it himself before school-leaving exams, from a familiar tree trunk from the forest. Whenever things didn't work out with a woman, he'd retrieve the dismountable bachelor's bed from his parents' attic, attach it in pieces to the roof rack of his white Mercedes with rubber straps and tarpaulin, prepared to drive into the next celibate phase of his life, which never lasted long. After someone like Johann, who held the passenger door of his car open like a Mercedes-wedding carriage, she had desperately sought Viktor. Just as she is seeking Johann now. Without the *how* in-between. Desperately seeking again, yet discreetly. Because a woman of fifty-four is rather an imposition on a thirty-six-year-old man, no?

Hello, there? Raoul asks, brushing a fly that doesn't exist away from her face.

You're still so young, she says, and her voice is husky, you still have a chance of winning the Nobel Prize in neurobiology.

So, if things don't work out here in Germany with a research career, Raoul repeats stubbornly, I'll just take off for Cuba again. He stands up and pushes the chair hard against the edge of the table. For a moment they stare at each other, each from their own side of the Formica tabletop, with the bitten-off roll that's simply clueless. In a moment Raoul will put on his headphones, which the boss doesn't like to see on people at work. The dangerous thing about listening to music is that it makes you think what's yet to be done has already been done, she reprimands whenever she catches young employees.

What do you want to do in Cuba then?

Accompany tourists in supervised drinking.

Raoul gets up to return his plate. The young woman is already standing there with her fists on her hips before batting the shabby yellow rag against a tray which clearly does not correspond with the graph-paper-like idea of hers as to the proper return of dishes.

Three times she strikes. Far away, close, past.

The sequence has something musical about it.


Wide-legged, Theres Grau swivels her desk-chair around once she returns to the office later that afternoon from a meeting at the Institute for Cancer Research. Theres gains momentum for another squeaky spin and, as she passes, points to the *Not a Rose* series, still leaning face forward against the cold radiator.

Does this artist actually get along with people?

Perhaps only with difficulty.

Flower disgraces, Theres says.

Do you want to nail the disgraces to the wall with me for our boss?

Theres laughs and looks as young as the day she introduced herself at the institute. On behalf of the boss, ever since Theres has been researching the connection between excitatory and inhibitory cells in the brain of mice, which allow conclusions to be drawn about human brains and their medical manipulability, on the other side of the corridor. The ultimate goal: immortality, even if no one talks about it in the corridors, not even to themselves. Theres' stinking mice are usually twelve weeks old, no longer young and already a little fat, when she anaesthetizes them, waits for them to breathe, makes the longitudinal incision in the abdomen, stabs them in the diaphragm and bleeds out the organs so that no disturbing haemoglobin in the mouse brain interferes with the research results. Then she cuts off the sleeping mouse's head. Theres started the mouse project in the lab over there three years ago. Mice stink. That doesn't change much, even if the pups are born from a germ-free gestation mouse, completely genetically manipulated and without a family nest. Over three years she's killed a thousand mice like this. Not nice, not nice, Theres had said at first, but that's the way it's got to be, that's the way it's got to be. Otherwise the brain cells won't live long enough, she'd said, and knotted the next headless animal body in an upturned disposable glove before disposing it in the bin under the sink. After a few months she smiled less and less and grew older around the mouth. Crooked and ever-more crooked she sat on her squeaky chair in front of the microscope. Lower and ever-lower she bent over the tiny mouse brains from which she took micro-thin slices. Her hair fell blonde onto her forehead as she made her way with fingers of light, as she liked to say, into a particularly beautiful brain cell, opening it up to observe the electrical behaviour of individual molecules and membrane proteins. But did Theres actually get any further in her day's work than an Augustine, 400 years after the birth of Christ? The fact that the sensory functions live in the brain just behind the face, but that memory lives towards the neck, and that a third place between the two controls all movements, was already proclaimed by the churchman more than one thousand six hundred years ago, without any research and dubious measuring methods. Biologically speaking, thoughts simply cannot be explained. Neither can feeling, sex or pain. And Theres Grau would not be able to reveal the secret of her soul with her fingers of light under a microscope either. She was unable to say whether during the process of death the water in the brain transformed itself into the pure wine of consciousness. Whether anything that remains is leftover. Actually, I like my work, Theres Grau often said, even if my fingers of light are actually paws in mittens. Yes, I like doing it, she repeats bravely to interns or visitors when they are allowed to look over her shoulder without having seen the limp remains of the mice in the rubbish first. Every cell, Theres then would say, has a character, has its own rhythm. Some are even beautiful, especially the interneurons; they are particularly beautiful and not as boring as the others. They are the conductors of thought, she says, but her voice sounds more and more preoccupied and not at all like music.

Could it be that Theres is sometimes afraid of her work? And if so, why?

Every answer is the colour of cement.

She watches Theres as she continues to spin on her squeaky office chair, working herself into a good mood.

Then she looks out the window behind the desk. A plastic bag has got caught in the tree there and held on. A plastic bag like a message. And blue. Who knows if a soul isn't drifting around in its wake, roaming once more through what used to be its home? With her back to it, Theres suddenly pauses. The chair squeaks, more quietly, then not at all. For a moment they stare out the window together, each entangled with herself over countless twists and turns of the brain, and as alone as innumerable plastic bags.

Quiet, Theres says and turns to her, What was that?

They both go out into the hallway and look. Just a row of other doors painted white but closed, three neon lights, an umbrella stand, five art prints. Nothing else. The corridor between the lab and the offices is deserted. At its end is the communal kitchen, a window bangs in the breeze. Shall I tell you something? a voice asks. What you haven't managed by your mid-thirties, you'll never manage again. Instead of an answer, there is a clatter of dishes that are being put into the dishwasher. She turns back to the half-open door. With the movement, the image of another half-open door emerges. Emerges behind what is, what once was. It is not her office she sees in the crack, but a cot with rumpled bedding and a story from way back when.

I was dead once, by the way, Theres, she hears herself say.

The white noise in her head droned through a Saturday evening, during the late film, which was as boring as *The Word on Sunday* that preceded it. Her mother was in bed, while grandmother had fallen asleep in her armchair. So had she, on a cheap runner in front of the TV. She woke up at the end of the programme. The TV screen was flickering white. She switched it off. The flickering remained, became a continuous noise, nestled in her head and had become even stronger by Sunday morning, swelling into a hiss that made Monday and the days that followed increasingly colourless. A heart attack in the head, a loss of hearing, her old paediatrician had commented, but one that comes from the brain, not the ear. She was sixteen and didn't go to school for weeks. Nina brought her homework. You're so weird, it's like you're wearing a raincoat all the time, joked Nina, and drove her to the hospital for outpatient treatment, where she collected her injection every day to be jabbed into the soft hollow between her neck and collarbone. Odd days on the right, on even days the left. One side of her face reddened until evening. First the right, the next day the left. One of the doctors was named Adler. On the Sunday morning she died, she saw a cot with rumpled bedding through the half-open door of the doctor's room. She'd fallen in love with this eagle who'd slept restlessly in that nest because it was too small for him. When he bent over her in the treatment room shortly afterwards, he was on duty for the third day in a row. She smelt alcohol, and not from the swab. Instead of saying something or quietly asking for help, she closed her eyes. The eagle missed. A plane crashed behind her closed lids. She jerked her eyes open again, but briefly, only to close them again on impact. The last thing she heard was a commotion in the room: We're losing her! My God, we're losing her . . . But she watched herself slowly take off the raincoat she had been wearing for the last few weeks. Underneath, she was already a little faded and as calm as if she had already departed. Naked, she entered a large marketplace in her mind where at the moment there was nothing. All around her was a flurry of snow, like a car ride in winter. She left this world, which was basically just cinders, because there was a much bigger beyond. She walked through snow, light and emptiness, seeing how her mind worked, how it dreamt, thought and left behind the place where once world had happened.

When she awoke, Nina was sitting by the bed, creaming her hands that lay on the bedspread like two dead birds.

What are you doing?

They brought you back with an oxygen tent and syringes to the heart, Nina replied, you were dead. Where were you?

Is that why you wanted to become a doctor and have something to do with the brain?

Theres Grau squinted a little when asking. Or is she just being serious?

Shortly after seven Theres and her walk through the automatic door of the institute which opens and closes again with a loud smacking sound. Until just a moment ago they'd been looking for a spirit level but, not finding one, in the end they just put the three pictures of Not-a-Rose back with their faces against the cold radiator. There are worse things that can remain undone in life.

And this friend, this Nina, what happened to her? Theres asks as they step outside into the last August sun.

Missing, she says.

Yes, Nina was missing since New Year's Eve. The disappearance of an adult woman was not a criminal offence, she once read in a police report—a woman could change her whereabouts without informing anyone. The most unbelievable things could happen that way. One day a man confessed to having murdered the missing woman, but then she turned up alive later, sometimes after three or thirty years later. It wasn't even sad any more, just eerie. In some cases the woman was still recognizable, but often she had become someone else, someone who hadn't had a bank account since the day she disappeared and had possibly only been to a doctor once, only when in dire need. She had long since been pronounced dead, and thereafter walked undisturbed by various pasts or the clamour of the present, but maybe she even made her way through the streets with a dog, past people who were all oblivious to her but had an opinion on the outcome of the last election or the bombings, impending wars, American or other presidents, or the glaciers melting.

Is your Nina that kind of missing person? Theres asks.

I think so, she says. When Nina walks the streets with a dog like that, the animal doesn't notice that she has nothing to say about world events. And if she doesn't think about any thing, the dog doesn't notice either.

Is that the case with your Nina?

I don't know, Theres, I think it's like that with me. I like dogs.

Why don't you have one?

I don't know. I don't have a husband either, though I like men.

Is that so? Theres laughs.

They walk to the bicycle stand. The saddles of the bikes are still warm from the August sun when they get on. At a bakery that is about to close, Theres buys a half-price roll for later. While waiting outside, she remembers a blue-and-red eraser on the folding table in her room, which Nina had left when dropping off her homework.

What's that about, Nina?

It was a Pelican eraser, one of those that quickly looked grubby and pitted.

Make something of it, Nina replies, take it and write a book with it.

A book? What kind of book?

One about forgetting.


It had been the dog's fault.

It was a terrier, Johann had said that early afternoon when he came home. They were in their seventh year living together, and his breath smelt of whisky. It would be their last year together.

Johann had wanted to avoid the terrier that had suddenly stood in the middle of the road and yelped as if he had personally issued a curfew on this stretch of a country road near Wesel. It had been raining for a few minutes and, because of the dog, Johann slid off the road and into a concrete bollard on which a potted Erica was standing. He had bought the yellow Fiat Doblò from a mechanic in the industrial area on the left bank of the Rhine, near Krefeld, who ran the workshop right next to his cheap barber. The next day he took up a new job. A salesman for books and stationery. Sometimes elderly ladies in the flat countryside would ask Johann if he could carry a parcel for them, they assumed the friendly driver of the yellow van was from the post office. Now the axle was broken. The police came and recorded the accident. It was the dog's fault, Johann had also told the officers. Even then his breath smelt of whisky.

Five days a week, Johann had driven the Fiat through western Westphalia and sometimes up and down the North Rhine country roads, where scrawny trees at the side of the road did little to hide the nothingness of the surroundings. He wore his old pike-grey suit. When it was still new, seven years ago at the turn of the millennium, she had torn open the sewn-up pockets.

To do what?

She didn't remember exactly.

On his sales tours, Johann had books and non-books in his assortment, mugs with and without inscriptions, erasers, napkins, postcards and other stuff that nobody needed but was offered anyway. Almost every bookseller was happy to earn extra money with knick-knacks. All too seldom did he pass museum shops on his routes, where he could listen attentively to well-ironed blouses and thus increase total sales among ladies over fifty by 20 per cent. His real clientele tended to be in the suburbs, where the city and its outskirts could hardly be distinguished from each other. Johann preferred to drive to old-fashioned stationery shops which did not yet have a post office next to the cash register. When he parked, he was already overcome by memories. Johann's mother too had a similar stationery shop in a small industrial town on Lake Constance. The town with its many one-way streets had smelt of Maggi and mustard sandwiches. Down by the River Aach, a little stream like a sigh, a one-armed man had told fairy tales to the children at the bathing area. Johann had sold workbooks to his classmates before eight in the morning, while his mother was still asleep in her girlish nightgown and with dirty dishes under the bed. She would rather have been a primary-school teacher than a mother.

That's how it all turned out. Johann did his Abitur instead of the planned apprenticeship as a heating engineer and ended up in theatre because of an opera singer, where as a dramaturge he sat in the canteen at the technician's table and rarely with the artists. Because when they talked and laughed, they opened their mouths as wide as horses at an auction. Or so he thought. Most of the time, at least. He'd also failed to reckon with the fact that the rooms where he would have to work in were often windowless.

Wouldn't it have been better if he had done an apprenticeship as a heating engineer? He was a salesman now. In friendly weather, Johann's left elbow hung out of the open side window of the yellow Fiat. A cigarette between his fingers, he felt like a cowboy once he stepped on the gas—a melancholy but chirpy cowboy accompanied by a torn-open bag of trail mix on the passenger seat. Sometimes she accompanied him instead of the bag.

Manuscripts piled up on the desk at home on the Wehrhahn. After editing a volume of lectures by her doctoral advisor—'Body, Space, Person. Outline of a Phenomenological Anthropology' —and doing a hell of a job on it, he'd gratefully recommended her to several academic publishers. She had quickly risen from a run-of-the-mill freelancer to a coveted freelance editor. She had not only managed to keep her head above water with her desk work but also was up-to-date with synchronous network activity of the brain, interdisciplinary research on consciousness and medical–ethical findings on brain death. Some days, however, she was glad to escape the violent ripples in the network of neurons, put on her old trainers, which were still from her time with Nina, and accompany Johann. She could take some time off and catch up on what she'd been neglecting at night or on Sundays. The fact that she had not become a practising doctor with a tight daily schedule also had its advantages. She could sunbathe in Johann the Salesman's car with the side window open while he disappeared behind some glass door. Once on one of these trips they talked about dignity. Dignity's just a word, Johann said, a fragile person full of self-doubt hiding behind it.

As a heating engineer, you'd certainly have been able to say the same thing, Johann.

Woulda', coulda', shoulda', he replied.

I didn't know you could argue so brilliantly, Johann.

He took a sharp turn, which he referred to as a come-to-me curve, pulled over to the side of the road, stopped and leant towards her without turning off the engine.

The fact is, it's always nicer to love you than not, Beautiful, he said. Once they'd stopped kissing, he added softly, it's a shame we don't have children, a real shame.

Really? nonplussed, she replied, looking down at her knees, two pale islands protruding pointedly from under the hem of her skirt. Really—what was that supposed to mean, thank you very much? There was a time when she'd thought that people could share an outer and an inner reality. They could communicate with each other if their outer realities were compatible. They could fall in love if their inner realities matched. But if the one's inner reality matched the other's outer reality then what they had was a secret, they belonged together without ever really belonging to each other. Even over distances, such people remained committed, she thought, while Johann turned the steering wheel again and drove back onto the road, the tyres squealing.

On the Saturday after the accident, Johann was sitting in front of the radio, drinking coffee from the old, white-on-red Hero-of-Labour mug. Its handle had been missing from the beginning, and it didn't bother him.

I won't burn my fingers that quickly!

At a time when the GDR was throwing away everything that reminded them of those forty years they'd been a country that threw nothing away, Viktor had rescued the cup from a rubbish bin on a trip to Havelland, outside of Berlin.

Johann was listening to a panel of experts on the radio talking about a book he'd bought the day before. The less money he had, the more he bought, especially cigarettes, shoes, whisky, books, paper towels and toilet paper. The panel was discussing how the author had made his way up from a working-class family to becoming a public intellectual. His storytelling was touching, dark, angsty and brilliant. Ah, Johann growled and poured himself some coffee while she gathered buckets and cleaning supplies and the change for the train. Outside the kitchen window, bright, papery clouds passed by, clueless. The Fiat was back at the mechanic's in Krefeld. Not a total loss, but not worth repairing, he had concluded, and had played a Bowie CD so that removing the seats wouldn't feel like a slaughter, but a positive farewell. She had waited for him next to the car. He was on the phone a few steps away with quizzical eyes. His old agency, Home to Home, rented out luxury flats to film productions, ambassadors and others who were in town only for a while and preferred flats with stucco near the Rhine. Whatever the cost. The agency needed cleaners like Johann who could also communicate with people in English and especially with those who had once been VIPs and were therefore even more sensitive. A lady from the agency neighed tenderly into the mobile Johann held away from his ear. She thought, Couldn't we just leave all of this and go somewhere else? But where, without any money? To the countryside, perhaps? Not that I'd want to become a country doctor in the end! No, I never jumped that particular train, and now it's left without me. But I could go through my manuscripts again and maybe even write something myself one day. About the gene for a better life that some people lack perhaps. A kind of experience-based report that has both: theory and authority. But then she thought, What would people like us be doing in the country? We're both afraid of free-range cows, the forest and the next dead zone.

A few steps away, Johann gestured slitting his throat at the end of the phone call. One day I'm going to put on a clown nose and start writing about all this, he said after hanging up. From the Fiat, with its driver's seat already removed, Bowie was singing something about heroes, heroes for a day. The screwdriver whistled along.

Why don't you write now, even without a clown's nose, Johann? she asked.

I do, I write every moment.

Can I read something?

Read? Not really, 'cause I write without actually writing, he replied.

Johann set his cup down on top of the radio. In a programme full of deep, thoughtful voices they were talking about a 'we' that lived in a world full of information but absent of any insight, surfeit with knowledge but meagre in experience. Who's this we supposed to be? Johann grumbled, all those who can't hold a spanner or a saw properly?

We are the ones who always knew but didn't understand, a voice from the radio answered, coughing into the microphone.

Did no one tell him that there is a throat-clearing button on the studio desk? Does he have to play the choking sheep in public? Johann said and lit his first cigarette before breakfast. He looked exhausted already.

We... he said again, and looked at her. Now he was coughing, too. We, she thought, we two are indeed a sad animal. She paused. It had been the same before. With another person at another time, but it felt the same. Like with Viktor? A moment of déjà vu? No, more likely a smack from an invisible hand on the back of her head, warning her: Watch out! Or soon you'll get cold.

She went to the bathroom and put on a patched, sleeveless vest for men and a pair of work trousers to accompany Johann to his cleaning job so he would actually go. Down the street she realized she had forgotten to brush her teeth.

All the same, the sun was shining.

They took the train across the city. She looked out of the window, then at the cleaning supplies Johann had placed between her feet as soon as they boarded. Across from them, a man in a fleece jacket that was too warm for this beautiful Saturday opened a newspaper. Liyuan Fu, he read aloud to the woman next to him, has distinguished herself as a police officer in China and on a foreign assignment in Kosovo to such an extent that she earned a Federal Chancellor Scholarship from among 100 applicants, which enables Chinese to pursue courses in Germany. She has been studying criminology in Ruhr University since February. It's just around the corner, the man said. Is that necessary? Who can keep track of all these Ping-Ming names here in this country?

Johann poked her. Yeah, is that necessary? he asked cheerfully and loudly, pointing out the window of the tram. Above the portal of a red-brick church hung a banner: Re-entry Possible at Any Time. I will never be able to leave this man, she thought. Suddenly it was there again, that familiar feeling of sitting together on the bonnet of the old white Mercedes, looking into the vagueness of a landscape, and being conspirators for the rest of their lives.

The train stopped. She reached for the cleaning kit. He fetched his book out of the bucket and tucked it under his arm.

And then it ceased, the feeling.

At the address, the doorbell only read APP 9. No name. Next to it the intercom. She and Johann had passed a playground on the way, where aged fathers were staring at swings. People sat on the pavements with juice and ice cream in front of cafes, enjoying themselves. No one was smoking. No one was looking at Johann or her or their cleaning bucket. No one in the neighbourhood seemed older than forty, and even if they were, they weren't conscious of it. She felt ashamed. We're just like you! she'd wanted to yell, we too are from the past millennium, just less efficient.

Johann pressed the bell while she took a step back and looked up at the building, which had something unpleasant about its elaborate, soppy, almost pathetic facade. Someone pressed the buzzer. Johann let her enter. On the first floor, a door opened, with flower vines etched on the glass at the top.

Where did this familiar fragrance come from?

She looked at the red sisal runner at her feet that led to the flat.

In front of the threshold was a new-looking doormat.

Was that a figment of her imagination now or a curious dose of remembering and forgetting that put that taste of cumin and orange on her tongue?

You?

She lifted her head.

A woman stood in the doorway.

*You*, she repeated.

The woman took a step aside and, as if in response, led into a flat whose corridor turned from one blink to the next onto a narrow strip of wasteland between a yellow villa and an eight-storey concrete abomination, where two girls, Nina and her, are stuffing their hands into their coat pockets during a storm, then running off and pumping their elbows, stumbling until—carried higher and higher by fabric wings or happy cries—they sail over wildly dumped rubbish up to the clouds. She remembered she had once wanted to go to the circus because Nina wanted to . . .

You here?

They stared at each other, each from their side of the doormat.

A late morning sun filled the hallway behind Nina with brightness. The floor had a chequerboard pattern of old tiles. On a Biedermeier dresser to the right was a vase of orchids of intense white. A small lamp with a yellow shade burned next to the bouquet. Come in. You're on time, my dears, Nina said, and it's great that you brought the cleaning stuff. Your agency didn't buy enough in time. She looked good and not all that surprised. Johann walked towards her but halted immediately.

A perplexed pawn who didn't know what might happen to him on the chessboard near the queen.

In the kitchen there was only a single, almost empty bottle of vinegar cleaner next to the sink. There was a mop in the broom cupboard, but no bucket. By the open fireplace in the living room, with a view of the old trees of an enchanted garden, a set of quick-drying synthetic bed linen hung on a clothes horse, and above the sofa was the poster of a Berlin exhibition from long ago, with Fidel Castro and his cigar on it.

She remembered a very different picture she had once torn out of a newspaper to write 'For Nina' on the back. In that photo from the '80s there were two girls who had climbed a courtyard wall. The one in jeans was already sitting on the crumbling top, pulling the blonde in the tight, dark skirt up by the elbows. You couldn't tell whether they were going to make it, but you could see that they were fond of each other.

At the time she thought, I would have loved to have taken such a photo myself. But what she really would have liked was to be part of the subject.

The picture of the two girls had been like a keyhole to her own inner images and had enriched her memory with the adventures of two completely different, completely unfamiliar other girls.

They started cleaning the kitchen, she and Johann, without exchanging a word. When the sound of an electric toothbrush came through the closed bathroom door, she took the bed linen off the rack in the living room and went into the bedroom. On the king-sized bed were two down blankets, without covers. Nina came out of the bathroom. She had changed and was now wearing a dark-blue dress with narrow white stripes at the cuffs and hem of the skirt and made a beeline for a Biedermeier wardrobe behind the hall door before putting on a raincoat despite the sunny weather.

A glance followed her, it lasted a few heartbeats too long and was thus a form of contact.

I'll probably be back in twenty minutes, she said, would you all like some coffee then?

Twenty minutes, the usual waiting time in dentists' consulting rooms, at night sometimes at bus stops or in restaurants. The world could change in twenty minutes. Some wars were shorter. Twenty minutes was seven rounds in the boxing ring. A theatre break was twenty-minutes long. In twenty minutes you could boil four eggs in a row, or focus your gaze on another person. Sex lasts twenty minutes on average. Twenty minutes had passed between the first and second impact of the two planes in the World Trade Center on 11 September 2001, almost six years ago.

She followed Nina towards the door without saying a word.

In twenty minutes the Biedermeier chest of drawers would reflect on a freshly mopped, shiny chequerboard floor, and the reflection would gradually disappear as the floor dried. Yes, a lot of things could happen in twenty minutes . . .

Nina waved and slammed the door. It was neither a loud slam nor a quiet pull. It had been like that before, too.

She went into the bathroom, saw the jeans and blouse Nina had just been wearing hanging over the radiator. She wrinkled her nose. The clothes smelt of caraway, orange and rosemary. There was a bottle of patchouli on the glass shelf under the mirror. Who even used that nowadays except for shamans and Nina?

Stuck to the white porcelain sink was an even whiter streak of toothpaste. She heard Johann working in the kitchen. Dishes were clattering. They were nice actually, such noises. In a better place than this they would be acoustic touches, caresses that said someone looks after you. You are not alone.

Coffee? Johann called out across the hall.

As she came into the kitchen, he was putting a silver moka on the stove. She sat down at the kitchen table. This can't be all that bad for you, you love watching horror films anyway, he said, especially when you're not feeling well, right?

She sat down across from him, and slid her arms over the tabletop until its edge bumped into her armpits. Hey, Johann said, hey now, don't worry, Beautiful, she won't be back in twenty minutes either.

Are you sure?

Quite sure.

Why?

She won't be back as long as we're here, Johann said.

**5.4**

At a construction site behind Zoo Station.

A young man steps out of the way for me on the narrowed pavement. Hair like raven's feathers and skin that's brown even without any sun. A thin blue rain jacket. Sleeves over his fingers. He is cold here. Despite it being spring. He gets on the bus to Tegel Airport.


**6.5**

Rainer Werner Fassbinder said that whatever you do should be a statement about the time in which it was made.


**13.5**

A dream: I am walking with my dog through a dark city. It is raining.

We arrive at a house. There are leaves in front of the door. I go in and immediately come out again. Don't you want to come in too? I ask the dog, who is lying wet on the wet leaves.

Later on the dog answers in a distorted voice, Later! I've still got something to do here. Besides, there's a storm coming.

**14.5**

Who doesn't want to find someone they can sleep on?

**23.5**

An architect, I read, who lived abroad for a long time and brought back not only languages but his view of the world, so, someone who was sent from city to city as a consultant for large building projects, who made the same 7.2 square metres disappear wherever he built, both in the plan and in the completed object. The empty space is what secures the building, I read.

I wonder if the new, expensive townhouse just a stone's throw from my old back building, the one that's so ostentatiously displacing air and light, remembers that it used to be an empty space once?

**17.6**

When he wants to talk about the past the Volvo driver who used to drive an Opel Kadett likes to talk about cars that were once small, square or even poppy-coloured. I remember that we used to record music from the radio on cassettes and hand them out like love letters, but not car brands . . .

And: Can you fall in love with old records again?
I ask the man who loves cars as he's about to
leave.


**1.7**

Why am I telling all these stories? Because it's
so easy to forget.

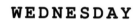

**WEDNESDAY**

Today is Wednesday.

Tomorrow is Thursday.

It's considered a little Friday. Some people already wish each other a nice weekend, as if they couldn't wait for time to pass.

The last time she saw Nina was over ten years ago.

Johann nine.

And Viktor?

A long time ago. Long.

Really?

How old is he now, anyway?

Eighteen years older than her, little will have changed over the last few years. Just what it was between them, she'd sometimes tried to talk about with Johann, but never to herself.

Or not really.

Robert Storm returns in three days.

He will be landing at Tegel Airport.

Storm is thirty-six.

She is fifty-four.

Numbers help tell stories. In ten years she will be sixty-four and, shortly after that, an old woman. Was she actually what is called a talented young woman years ago? Talent alone doesn't form character.

True, she says quietly as she descends the escalator of a department store with a packet of espresso in her hand, picking at the price tag and, arriving at the foot of the stairs, takes the next one.

If more had been possible in her life, what could it have been? A better position, money, children, a quiet house and the even quieter happiness of being in firm, friendly hands? Johann's hands or those of someone like Storm.

Johann knew her well.

Not knowing Storm had its advantages.

Had she fallen in love?

And even if she had indeed, what did that have to do with him?

No one can forbid her to turn his absence into images of presence. Everyone has such narrative imagination. Every brain thinks in stories. No one can prevent her from talking to this Storm in one or the other part of her own brain, telling him about her life, and thus reinventing herself for him. While on the escalator, she observes the clientele of the ladies' department aimlessly dawdling between branded boutiques. Storm is now as old as Johann and Viktor were when she knew them. Which doesn't mean that she can now get to know Storm better. Yes, perhaps talking to him will always remain a monologue but one she will remember as a tender exchange between the two. She can boldly or cockily direct his non-existent attention towards the woman she never was but could have been. A person becomes a narrator especially when that speck of inner nothingness, which isn't yet boredom, opens up. She knows that. People share stories of their lives in a way that even the worst catastrophes take on some meaning.

She knows that too.

And isn't that how all love stories begin?

Perhaps.

Even a potato can be part of an autobiography.

Can a potato be a warm bed, too?

Yes.

And head nurse Anna?

She moves on to the next escalator.

To be honest, the woman who had clogged into her life in healthy, well-worn eggshell-coloured shoes back then wasn't a catastrophe. She'd smelt of rubber and dust, of Nivea and dandruff, of foot sweat, too, and the smell of stale coffee from her mouth.

And she wasn't a disaster?

No. Just a dragon.


This is not a hotel, Miss, this is where people come to die, head nurse Anna had said at her interview in 1981. How old are you again? What, only a perfect 0.9 grade on your Abitur? You poor thing, with a school-leaving certificate like that you have no choice but to study medicine, do you? Have you ever worked in a hospital? We pay 7.23 marks an hour, including a dirty-work bonus and Berlin allowances. After all, we're pretty far east, even though we're in West Berlin. This really isn't a nice job, Fräulein, head nurse Anna declared, and she was terrifying.

She, the young Fräulein, had only been living in Berlin for a few months when she started cleaning the faces of old ladies with terrycloth flannels, noticing the closing of the eyes—

which seemed like practicing death—when she washed their ears, necks, décolleté, armpits, arms, hands, chest, stomachs and genitals, as well as their thighs and feet, listening to the soft snowing in the old ladies' heads. The disease, she well knew, could start with socks in the fridge and you having no idea how they got there. At first you still ask yourself, What's going on? What's wrong with me? Later on the questions—and then the self-talk—begin to peter out before going silent altogether. But the senses remain. And in the end life passes by like that of the trees outside the window.

Yes, she quickly got used to the veins and bumps of old skin, the musty smell of the scalp. She got used to switching on the light in the morning in the darkened room, got used to her own warm matter-of-factness in asking the ladies what they had dreamt in the night before switching off the overhead light again so that the day could tiptoe into the room while she washed. She was the only one who did it that way. Her colleagues preferred the merciless, buzzing ceiling light because the stockings they had to put on the women after they finished their toilet were always too wide. Because the women spread their fingers, making it difficult to put on their bed jackets. They felt fragile to the touch, these women, even if they were fat, like Ms Thesky, who one morning repeated, Thank you, thank you, thank you before digging her finger into the cut roll. Thank you, back at home I didn't eat any more but now I'm quite healthy, but tell me, Queen Louise, and tell me, you fucking queen you, you cunt, have you been fucking all night again in your black stockings? As far as her neighbour Stumpfögger was concerned Thesky didn't recite dirty words, but incomprehensible poems to which she'd beat out the rhythm on her bedspread.

Until one night Stumpfögger struck back.

With the plastered arm she had broken while in the shower.

At the beginning she'd waved it at everyone who came into the room while happily calling out a-missnatch-a-missnatch, I'm-a-seventeen-year-old-blonde—but by the end of the week none of her sons had come back to visit. Then on Sunday night Stumpfögger must have stumbled over something in her head that came undone. A birdcage, she said later, she'd left in a cold hallway for far too long, decades ago, when she wanted to look for fresh bird sand somewhere else. While searching for the bird sand, she'd forgotten about the bird and that was the one she had wanted to look for seventy years later. She heaved her forty kilos out of bed, raised her axe-like casted arm and set off. The first thing she did was hit Ms Thesky so she would finally stop with the poems and all the talk about fucking. The next room-mate got a blow to the head for her snoring. And so Stumpfögger went on, thrashing from bed to bed until, on her fifth strike, the hated cast finally broke.

She changes escalators and remembers: Stumpfögger, still quite limber for an eighty-seven-year-old, had sat on the floor and scratched her freed arm bloody . . .

Quite the story, and you don't have any idea when to cry and when not to laugh at all. Do you? She looks at the steps of the escalator in front of her.

They are empty.

The fact that Storm is not here and she is not there makes a third place, just as a negative multiplied by a negative makes a plus. She has just felt him next to her. And what one has felt is what one has experienced. She knows that, too. From life and from science. That's why she became a neurobiologist. Neuro-biology is her strategy to gather herself together. Especially when things are not going her way, she looks for a scientific explanation for feelings of grief and dejection. This way she can observe life as well as herself from a distance and get a better perspective.

Looking closely can also be comforting?

Yes, it strengthens the immune system.

Indeed, she remembers.

One day she came home from school and said to her grandmother: Come on, tell me I feel pain! They had just gone over nerve pathways in the spinal cord in biology class, and afterwards she had sat down all alone under an apple tree and realized that all her sensations were just signals from the brain.

One last time she changes the escalator, gets on the one towards the ground floor. As the steps level out in front of her, a little boy jostles past her then turns around, smiling broadly, his hair sticking out and his face full of freckles. Storm's son? Then the boy runs across the perfume department after a woman with long dark hair and holding a little girl by the hand. Storm's wife and children? Once the woman turns towards her. She looks lovelier from the front than from behind. Suddenly the boy points to a man. He comes towards the three of them and spreads his arms. The children run to him and the four of them make their way towards the underground car park.

She looks around. There are young boys everywhere. All of them look like Storm.


What's wrong with you? her boss asks when her best employee arrives late because of a packet of espresso.

What's the matter? Drifted away with your thoughts?

A blue binder is waiting on the desk. 'Neurogenesis, Or Why Vampires Never Grow Old' on its cover.

Your face, the boss says.

What about it?

Oh, says the boss, it's just me. I can't go into an art gallery any more without diagnosing the people that've been portrayed.

She pushes the binder back and forth on the desk as if looking for better lighting on stage. Lectures by the boss in which the word 'neuro' appears in the title are well-paid and popular among managers of car companies who are obsessively interested in immortality before they snap out of it. All these gentlemen in suits who look like they were raised in airports hang on the lips of the beautiful boss at the latest when she tells them about parabiosis: A young and an old mouse are sewn together in an experimental operation so that two blood circuits become one and the two animals become conjoined with two heads, eight legs and two hearts. The aim of this union is to stop the ageing process. The experiment promises life on the edge of eternity, even if one forgets about the future there, and in the end the words only come out with difficulty, but the saliva runs down the chin . . .

Hello, the boss says, you know what, my dear? For years, whenever I look at you, I've thought your name could actually be Konstanze. Konstanze, the steadfast one. Today, for the first time, I don't think so. What would you really like to be called?

Olga, she promptly answers.

Olga, the boss repeats, immersed in thought.

When she was thirty and desperately wanted to change her first name, she and Viktor had tried 'Olga' for a holiday in Italy. Viktor played along, but she didn't respond when he called her. The following year, as a nude model at an art academy, she actually introduced herself as Laura, but never realized she was the one they meant when they said, Laura, go ahead and get dressed again. She remained stock-still. One day Viktor suggested the name 'Isabelle'. She didn't even say no, just looked away.

That morning the wire coat hanger in Viktor's room had lain on the light carpet in front of the roll-top cabinet, the wool as tall as unmown grass.

Had it been because of the curious feeling she had dragged from the night before into the morning, the feeling she had nicknamed Ostende? Or her fantasy that Viktor had been tamed between light sleeping and deep waking and had become a woman beneath her, while she moved those few centimetres towards or away from him that thing called love? Of course, Viktor hadn't worn an old purple petticoat that night and had long been shaved, showered and gone by the time she woke up that morning and wandered alone through his flat.

He didn't intend to be back before evening.

She had bent the wire hanger into a hook and slid it into the keyhole of the roll-top cabinet like a pick. Pushed it in again and again. She later remembered this action—tinged with fear and with desire—exactly, but not the reason for it. As she twisted, pushed and pulled, the room transformed. Even the air suddenly seemed crooked.

Was that the moment she decided never to get married?

She no longer knew.

Where did your memories go when you didn't have them anyway?

In the end, she was surprised at how easily the lock gave way and the slats rattled down loudly while she stood wrapped in her bath towel, arms hanging wearily by her side, envelopes sliding towards her from the compartments, wrapped in brown paper bag.

Isabelle, Paris, 1972
Anna-Clara, Albania, 1973
Anna, Recklinghausen, 1975

Karin, Recklinghausen, 1975 / 78

Viola, Berlin, 1980

Angela, Leipzig, 1980

Annalisa, Milan, 1981 . . . 1981, that's NOW, she thought, staring at the years, places and first names where the addresses should have been. Some names appeared twice. Heike, Sabine or Brigitte. Brigitte, her mother had once said, Brigitte, that's not really a name, just a collective name for women of a certain generation.

One bag was unlabelled. She looked into it first: photos of women, most of them in colour and of no particular technical ability. It was a little helpless, sinking-to-the-floor feeling which helped her settle down in front of the cabinet, as if she'd forgotten how to stand.

Goodness, girls, you could've put on a bit more clothing . . .

Even if the women were beautiful, there was something sordid about the pictures, as if they showed their subjects in a moment that had been wrested away, only to become embarrassing later on. Most of the pictures were from the '70s. The women were naked or just about naked. Lolling about on patchwork quilts they might have crocheted themselves, backs rested, knees spread, mouths half-open, wearing bridles from the sex shop, suspenders, thongs, see-through push-ups, everything made of cheap mist. They undid little leather jackets with nothing underneath, walked naked along the sea, offered a dog a thick plastic carrot to play with in front of an open fireplace as a breast slipped out of a T-shirt and a string of hair appeared on a face. Or onto a man's belly and they had themselves photographed like that, a torso-length away from the photographer and his hand on the shutter release, while they pleasured him with hand and mouth, still seeming to laugh or cry with their mouths full. It depended on the size of each woman's mouth. Or on the viewer?

In one photo a young woman was sitting on a bicycle. The shot was taken from behind, her one foot on the ground, one on the pedal, looking over her shoulder at the camera. Her short skirt was hiked up. Her bare bottom flashed at the hem as she stuck out her smile. In the background, the blurry outlines of a harbour and two Gothic church towers.

Ostende?

Sorry, she muttered, putting the photos back in their envelopes and the envelopes into the bottom of the cabinet. Then she opened the two drawers. In one was a pair of black leather trousers, in the other a stack of black notebooks with red edges. She took the one on top and leafed through it. The entries were from the current year.

13.3.82 She's nice, the girl from Zoo Station, but . . .

She paused. She heard something at her back, footsteps trying not to be heard. Turning around, she saw Viktor standing in the doorway. His laughter sounded like the call of a peacock as their eyes met. Something about him moved her, something else did not.

He raised his hand and three fingers. I swear, he said.

Then he was no longer there, gone and out of the flat and the building. She didn't move, not even when the door slammed shut. There had been neither a loud slam nor a quiet pull. From the window she saw him running across the rain-soaked yellow paving stones of the church square like an injured animal ready to strike.

Suddenly, on either side of his path, forest. There were conifers standing close together, and the dark shadows between them. It was a long, dead-straight but narrow road, there was something hypnotic about the rows of trees straggling towards each other at mid-distance at the crowns.

In the evening Viktor returned. He brought a bottle of white wine and two frozen pizzas from the supermarket. His hair was freshly cut. They ate, drank, talked and slept together. Afterwards they laughed. In late autumn we'll go to Italy, he had said. And when they did, the country was just like he had promised. Roads cutting into a wilderness that led to deserted, grass-covered vineyards which were soon followed by throngs of fruit trees, vine-covered figs and cherries, as well as willows, plane trees, elders and acacias, until the ascent to the sky began in earnest, through dark hornbeam and poplar with light once again at their hem, less heaviness and more familiar plants if mixed in with foreign ones like oleander, cypress and other fairy tale-like trees that could give an unexpected clearing the mood of a wasteland even though a scent of hot, breathing asphalt or fresh mortar permeated the air, a smell that said cars might be nearby, down there, on a coastal road by the sea.

Did it mean anything at all, what they had together?

He could inscribe memories into her head that she soon thought were her own, having forgotten the moment of contagion.

Viktor was a flexible person with an unyielding heart. They never talked about the roll-top cabinet again. Get used to it, she said to herself, get used to your shame and his. Get used to feeling offended when he doesn't want to take such photos of you in the weeks or months to come. Get used to it, get used to the fact that your story didn't actually start on a 13th of March in front of Zoo Station, but much earlier. In Ostende when Viktor was twenty-one and you were three. Your story began when you knew nothing about each other. Get used to the fact that the little salesgirl will often be with you at night, like an angel making strange noises, crying in the bathroom, yawning in the kitchen or standing by the window, smoking. Get used to the angel who turns to the two of you as soon as one of you sighs or groans and says monotonously into the darkness: I am not completely burnt. I am making my way through other spaces. I am walking through your dreams.

Why did she stay with him?

The next morning Viktor sent her back to Berlin. She didn't have a return ticket yet, and he didn't buy her one but drove her to the next motorway exit. She would hitchhike to Berlin. Even as she was approaching the first driver of a lorry with Berlin plates—who gave her a lift right away and later even shared his homemade schnitzel sandwiches in the cab—Viktor had already turned around and driven off.

The Ostende feeling remained.

As did she. She stayed on for the next fifteen years.

Why?

What was significant?

For a long time she felt as if they carried each other's burden. And that made them companions.

The mystery inherent in the beginning of every love story did not wane between Viktor and her in later years. It only magnified the space between them. It seemed that because of this void love also remained like a side effect of the mystery. Ever since she had seen the photos, she'd suspected that Viktor had put together pictures of the women the way he himself would have wanted to be the one photographed.

Did Viktor desire to become a woman?

Did she want an answer?

She would never know what kind of oath Viktor had made that day in the doorway to the room with the roll-top cabinet. Maybe he'd just thought, This isn't how our story ends. Let's just move on, and she had unspokenly agreed. She had known: I am not the love you crave, but simply the one who's here. Nevertheless ... Viktor would come up with the subject of her doctoral thesis and many years later say: Write about us, write about emotional contagion. Examine what you want to say with some clinical objectivity. Expand the title, call it 'Emotional Contagion in Healthy, Depressed and Schizophrenic Patients'. She would complete a doctorate in medicine, aware that the brain is a relational organ and what is so easily called warmth describes a personal, subjective sensation, but the movement of physical particles as well.

Viktor himself had never thought of working on his own doctoral thesis, even though in their shared history he'd been the gifted, skilful, curiously knowledgeable one.


I hope you like my vampire text, Konstanze, and that it'll quickly be proofread. The boss stops in the doorway to watch her colleague leaf through the manuscript and bring a few unruly ends of hair into shape with her conductor's hands before going out into the daily lab routine.

Yes, I like this one. A lot.

What?

She reads: It is enough at the moment to understand the brain as it is, will we one day be able to explain even purely subjective experience with the effect of molecules and brain structures? I am sure we will. It will be a happy coincidence that will make it possible. Only I won't live to see it ...

What are you smiling at? her boss asks, what do you like about it?

The me.

Sorry?

She looks at her boss. Sure, once upon a time they could both sing and dance and maybe were even considered beauties. But only one of them probably had the right mother. The other one, the one with the wrong mother, now raises her hand and plays with her hair, too. But do what they will the tips just will not grow wavy, for either the successful one over there or the one who never became a practising doctor for fear of patients over here. But they both have worries. They can be counted by the hair that fall out in the brush every morning. The more worries, the more risk of hair fall. They could both be lacking vitamins or something else entirely.

She smiles: That the author says 'I' at the end of the manuscript, I like that very much, Boss.

She was at Tegel Airport for the first time in her life. Yellow bucket seats divided the main hall and stood back-to-back in the aisle. She tossed the green duffel bag onto the seat next to her and looked at the display clacking away with changing departures and arrivals. Moscow, Zurich, Istanbul . . .

An elderly man pushed a rack of postcards next to his newspaper display and went off to carry back another golden umbrella-shaped stand. A silly thing in which he arranged plastic, see-through children's umbrellas like flowers. A woman in grey overalls with shoulder pads and neon stripes on the side seams stopped and pulled a bank note out of her breast pocket.

Looking at her from the side you could see she was pregnant.

I need you!

Oh, let me sleep, Viktor, she said into the receiver of the new push-button telephone that night in her Rote Insel neighbourhood. Let me sleep, Viktor, in three hours night will be over. I've got the early shift.

I need you, he'd repeated.

They need me, too, Viktor.

Theirs had become long-distance relationship, with long calls after midnight when the rate was cheaper. The telephone cord was extra-long because between them was a transit route from West Berlin to Helmstedt, and then a long stretch of A1 to the edge of the Ruhr. In purely mathematical terms, a distance of 526 kilometres, if she didn't count the eighteen-year age difference. She looked for the lamp next to the mattress. The numbers on the alarm clock lit up. Shortly after three.

Come on, I'm almost forty, Viktor said.

You don't die of that.

My wife is dead.

Your wife, she repeated, realizing she didn't even know her name after all these years.

The mattress was on the floor. She pushed herself up and switched on the light of an old desk lamp that stood beside the bed. Next to it lay the book.

*The Devil in the Flesh* by Raymond Radiguet. One of Viktor's recommendations.

She'd seen his divorced wife two or three times. The woman had joined the Communist Party at fourteen. That was another reason why he'd married her. She was blonde. A good remedy for boredom in Viktor's eyes. Every first Saturday of the month she came over to cut his hair. The visitor from Berlin then left the flat and resolved never to come back, only to stand in front of the door again after three hours at the latest, and to stop herself from saying two things.

Did you two fuck?

And:

I can cut hair too!

At the end of those Saturdays, Viktor would turn his back to her. On the door that was his bed, he would let his hand wander up the pile of old newspapers as if it were his personal archive, and not hers. And that was how he sent her away, even if she was allowed to lie next to him. She would have been home in half an hour—just a bus and train ride away—with her mother and grandmother in the eighth-floor flat with the satellite dish. But instead, on such afternoons, she preferred to wander aimlessly around Viktor's hometown between chimneys, church towers and closed shops, like a dog he'd set out in front of the door. Behind the fogged-up windowpanes of cafes, old women in hats sat at round tables, drinking from blurred cups with blurred faces. Although the image was peaceful, she couldn't help thinking of a city under siege, of Belgium or a makeshift tent at the edge of the world. Halfway up the slope, perched above the city was Viktor's university, in haze, mist or rain. Just like Ostende. And she would lay next to him on those Saturday nights as if she wasn't there. From the movements of his fingers along the pile of old newspapers, she was allowed to read the depth of his sleep. A sound, similar at first to the unobtrusive, continuous whirr of the fan, which swelled until it became space in itself. When she looked up from her bed in this new-formed space, there was no longer a ceiling above her. The sky arched in a vast arc, yawning down on her back, untouchable, and she realized in the second before she fell asleep how large the so-called bed where Viktor slept really was.

Come on, please, Viktor protested on the other end of the telephone line to Berlin, while she was already stumbling through her room and just about breaking a toe because of the long telephone cord. She fumbled her way into the kitchen. The window to the inner courtyard was open. On the same floor in the side wing opposite—where Viktor would soon be pulling scratchy porn magazines out of the ash tray of a green-tiled stove and crookedly and clumsily hammering a few nails into the wall— she saw her neighbour and her mother sitting at the kitchen table eating in their bathrobes like two outcast goddesses. Sourcream cake or polenta with butter and salt? The women were from Siberia and always ate at night. During the day the mother would knit while the daughter worked downstairs at the brothel. Their one-and-a-half-room flat was cut like her own, only in reverse. But in hers there was no table in the kitchen where a mother would sit and eat. An old bathtub on a wooden pedestal she'd made herself and a fat kitchen buffet she'd rescued from a container took up all the space. She set the phone down on the windowsill and pulled out a glass from the dishes soaking in the tub. There was no sink or washbasin either. She clamped the phone between her ear and shoulder, held the glass under the shower head and ran water. Again she looked at the women in the window opposite. Siberia, she thought, can be quite nice too. If it's more the people than the country and you managed to gather all the love in one place around you, then you could probably bear it in Siberia . . .

I'll buy you a flight, Viktor whispered, 526 kilometres away.

Sorry?

She turned off the water and looked at the gas boiler where a small flame was burning, a flame like an eternal light, only in blue.

OK, she replied standing in her kitchen that night, running her finger up and down the edge of the bathtub, OK, I'm coming. Are you going to pick me up?

I've never flown before, she'd said to the woman in the grey overalls who had joined her on the yellow bucket seats. Between them the duffel bag lolled green.

The woman was indeed pregnant. She was nibbling the price tag off a child's umbrella that she must have bought at the airport kiosk.

You're really pale, it's the fear of flying.

You're really pale . . .

The woman slipped one hand under her belly and put the other on the duffel bag. Tenderly, somehow. For a moment the duffel bag seemed like the head of a child. My goodness, what were those glorious spots that some god had sown on her face so that she would reap only joy? Not only was it full of freckles, but it was also full of bright speckles of light that the morning sun cast on her skin through the glass roof of the airport's main concourse. The hair the woman had tucked behind her ears, the flash of her long earrings, the shadow of light in the neckline of her blouse were like an offer.

She pointed to the woman's belly, over which the button placket of the grey overalls stretched.

Boy or a girl?

A boy for sure.

Quite sure?

The belly is pointed, that's a good sign. I'm in shape, that's great, too. Girls rob their mothers of beauty during pregnancy and make them fat as sausages. Boys don't . . .

And what's the boy's name going to be?

Robert.

Like the boy from *Shockheaded Peter* who flies away with his umbrella?

That's right, with the umbrella in the storm, said the pregnant woman, poking the tip of the little umbrella between her toes sticking out of her sandals. Just like a real Robert Storm...

On the displays for arrival and departure, city names, flight numbers, times and gate numbers changed their positions, clacking. The flight to Viktor was the seventh.

I've got to go, she said, say hello to Robert for me once he's landed happily with you.

Thank you, said the pregnant woman, maybe we'll see each other again some day.


When she arrived two hours later she put the green duffel bag down between her and Viktor who was running his hand over his face so that she could hear his three-day beard. Everything around her was overlaid with the rasping stubble, as if she had a Walkman on and had to construct whole new contexts of meaning between vision and sound.

I'm sorry about your wife.

Viktor watched a woman wearing a washed-out T-shirt go past. Good that you're here, he said. The green duffel bag between them tilted against her thigh, as if it wanted to think in peace.

The worst thing were the burns on her head, he said a few minutes later while holding the car door open for her. The bridge of her nose and forehead were the only things that still shimmered like skin through a burnt blueberry pie that had once been her face.

He tossed the green duffel bag onto the back seat.

Lying on the floor, she'd hid under the pillow to protect herself until it slid to the side, Viktor said. When the police found her, she looked as if someone had smeared her with caramel before pulling a pair of defective fishnet tights over her.

He started the engine but did not drive off immediately.

The cat, in any case, managed to escape through an open window.

Your cat's gone?

Yeah.

Where were you when she died?

Not there.

They both stared at each other, each from their own side of life.

On the day of the funeral the cat returned. Seven months later Viktor moved to Berlin. I'm going to write a book there, he declared, maybe buy a little house or plant a garden with you.

But first he rented the flat on the second floor in the side wing opposite hers. Overnight, the mother and daughter had disappeared. Probably to Siberia. Now, Viktor and she were a short distance apart, just a sad back courtyard with a few square metres of sky above it.

She took charge of the renovation but didn't touch the green-tiled stove in the big room. It probably didn't work any longer anyway. She put up radiators, cleared a pigeon's nest from the balcony and swabbed the toilet, and then an old refrigerator that hummed like a diesel engine as part of the furnishings next to the cooker. She took the jar of pickled vegetables and the leftovers from the salted cod over to her place. She went to the D-I-Y store with a friend who studied sports and was passionate about handball. They walked up and down between rolls of carpet, he in one aisle, she in the other, among the special offers. Needlefelt seemed to be a good floor covering.

In the evening, she and her friend laid the felt for Viktor. Brecht's *Downfall of the Egoist Johnann Fatzer* was playing on the radio. When her friend—enthralled by the punk music between the scenes—wanted to take a break, she lay down next to him.

Tell me, why can't your man renovate this place himself? he asked. Is he senile already?

No love, no love story either, not even a story, she said to herself as she and her friend rolled apart again twenty minutes later. Her back burning from the freshly laid felt. He ran his finger along it, murmured 'construction site' to the wound and kissed it.

That's what you get when you don't want someone in your bed.

In the meanwhile the credits of *Fatzer* were playing. She went into the kitchen and got some beer from the fridge. For a moment she paused with the handle in her hand before reaching for the two bottles in the door compartment, felt as if she were bending over herself. There was a sudden noise in her head, a continuous din she already knew. When it happened the first time, she had tried to ignore it, this white noise that had been a warning sign even then, albeit imperceptibly quiet like the first crack of an iceberg on the belly of a deep-sea steamer.

A week later Viktor set up his desk on the felt she had chafed her back and put down a woven rug that at some point must have soaked up a lot of sun.

More Morocco than Ostende.

He pushed the roll-top cabinet against the wall opposite. She leant her forehead against the windowpane. What kind of sad windows were those over there, on the second floor opposite? When there was sun on this side, it was dark there. Viktor stepped up to the window beside her, brushed her hair and kissed the back of her neck. She stood stock-still. Had she never had it better with anyone else?

She'd had it much better.

*Frisson érotique*, he said, seeing her goose flesh. She didn't dismiss him.

Ostende at this time of day was certainly quite chilly, cloudy and damp.

Viktor would teach architecture at a university of applied sciences near Zoo Station. He didn't really like architects per se. Quite select personalities, he said, but I prefer working with such herds of unique characters. Somehow I need these academic show-offs constantly making a scene about all they lack.

At the interview he had wowed those present with his statements on the depth of the world, the expiry date of realities and the associated decay of an old space. He ended his lecture with the cryptic statement: Everywhere is Sardinia, when you sleep alone. While doing so he had looked at the only woman in the committee and knew he had the job in the bag.

The university of applied sciences that brought him away from the concrete cathedral on the edge of the Ruhr to West Berlin offered him a position in architectural theory, which enabled him to make extensive excursions into aesthetics, sociology and politics, too.

Yes, Viktor liked to make excursions.

Five years later, the Wall fell.

**13.7**

By the rubbish bins.

Last winter, on the morning of New Year's Eve, four pale boys stuck red explosives into a snowman's cold white flesh and blew him to bits, although they'd built one themselves the year before.

Terror!

So now, in July, by the bins, I meet an actress who has recently moved into the front building. She lifts the lid and says: May I hold it for you?

Thank you!

Two floors up, the actress makes a phone call with the window open as soon as it's warm. Then, enveloped in her voice, I walk across the inner courtyard, more slowly than usual. I'm in a Fassbinder film.


**15.7**

Milky day at the sea, with mosquitoes, thin rain. I will be here longer now. Came here in the Volvo Man's Volvo and am looking after a house.

No, not his.

A neighbour is mowing his lawn as if he were going to war, while a local cat snores in my bookcase.

**17.7**

How does a lake feel when it rains?

In any event, puddles are islands for fish, Kluge said.

**19.7**

Such beautiful weather, and I'm there too. Who else said that? Someone on a balcony up on the eighth floor?

**20.7**

The neighbour brings cucumbers. From now on I'll call him the Cucumber Man. His sprinkler gives a rhythm to the silence.

And otherwise?

Tastes like the pistachio ice-cream of yesteryear, the day, the summer, this piece of the year and, later, the memory of it too.

**25.7**

Next door, some very young chickens are clucking in the coop. They have rather striking feathered coiffures. Evenings the Cucumber Man sits by the cage with his wife. The fire bowl is burning. The chickens have long been asleep, but the party voice of the wife who looks like a cat on two legs, crows all the way over to me. Hearing him too, I know they're no longer sober. Then they go straight to sleep.

Once, in the Eifel, I stroked a tame chicken and stared at strangers. Is that why the house by the lake now reminds me of the Eifel?

**26.7**

We're going out to dinner tonight, says the cat on two legs.

Where to?

To Potsdam. To McDonald's.

**29.7**

Years ago, everything was different here. The butcher's wife knows.

The postman walks too upright.

And what was the Pickle Man?

**30.7**

The Pickle Man used to be an electrician, I learn. He maintained the border fence between East and West. In front of the entrance to his garage he has set up a small table with a small pumpkin, the first of the season, a few tomatoes and, of course, some cucumbers. From my own harvest—please help yourself written on a handmade sign.

**1.8**

I drive back into town. As I slam the boot of my borrowed Volvo shut, a chicken answers with

Dido's death aria from Purcell's opera. The chicken is certainly sporting an even more dramatic hairdo than usual.

But no pain of separation. It has only laid one egg.

And: a few hours later, it's already night, I'm walking through a cemetery.

On one grave there's a plastic petrol station, on the one next to it a miniature World Trade Center. I have passed both graves and there is a rustling behind me. I turn around. On the grave with the World Trade Center the earth is rising like black roofing felt. Someone throws a bone at me, which in the dream is reddish and very even.

Almost like a drainpipe.


**2.8**

Where will the cat snore from now on?

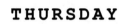

**THURSDAY**

That film evening at Theres' little end rowhouse she'd finally got her way. To her, Rainer Werner Fassbinder's *World on a Wire* was the best thing he ever did in his short life. Every shot, every gesture, every word spoken as if from under a thin raincoat says that there really is no such thing as reality. When Fassbinder died thirty-seven years ago at thirty-seven, the others there in Theres' living room in front of the beamer hadn't even been born, but she and Viktor had been together for a year. During these film evenings, she is the only one who never sits on the floor.

Should we keep on watching till next Thursday? Daniel asks.

How many episodes are there? Mike wants to know.

Two, she replies.

Only two? Raoul asks.

Yes. I've already seen them both.

When?

At the beginning of the '70s.

Theres Grau, in slippers, pours more wine and asks, How old were you?

Ten or so.

They let you do that?

They did.

I can't believe it!

I had a TV in my room.

What kind of family was that? Theres, outraged.

Mine, that is, not much of one.

For a long time she thought she'd made up memories spending two evenings in front of the yellow sphere TV with sardine sandwiches on her lap. When she asked around, nobody had seen *World On a Wire* except her. Not even Nina. No one had even heard of it. Had the story about the man named Stiller been broadcast just for her and a couple of oily sardines, her witnesses? That fit. *World On a Wire* played on the assumption, or fear, that reality does not exist. What looked like experience or life to Stiller did not happen to him, was nothing but the function in a giant computer that received signals and fired on, similar to the human brain. So the film—which according to the credits had been made, or not made, by someone named Fassbinder—had also only taken place in a single child's TV-set, or worse, in a lonely child's head, which was also only a circuit in a computer? If what the film said was true. And how lonely it was! Really, nothing real at all? But a negative multiplied by a negative equalled a positive, she knew that much from school. But so what did not-real times not-real equal? A nothing that nobody wanted but which was worth a message to the universe, which played it back on a single spherical children's TV-set, even if this TV-set and the underage viewer in front of it with the sardines on her lap didn't exist either. Later, when she thought of the Fassbinder film, she realized it had lodged itself in her mind like all good films do. It wasn't the plot that was important, but the feeling she had while watching it. It said you can be very alone even if you don't exist. That's what it's like. Death.

In *World On a Wire*, Stiller was trying to solve the death of a staff member at an institute about which little was known except that it had a lot of security. Stiller lived in a small town. Just like hers. Fish of light in the puddles of nocturnal streets were his only allies. After each of his attempts to solve the crime, the world was left more mysterious than before. But he was getting to the bottom of himself. Stiller discovered that the man named Stiller did not exist at all. Stiller was an identity unit in a computer called Simulacron, was a simulation, something he could have guessed if he had wanted to read the world around him more closely and hear the voices of the things in it more clearly. They said, Don't take me as a guarantee that there is reality here, Stiller, just because I am a real object. Stiller suspected all this. Which was more agonizing than knowing it. Take it easy, Stiller, she had said to the TV, had pushed the plate of oily sardine sandwiches off her lap and looked around. Neither the green curtains in front of the plastic blinds at the window, nor the striped wallpaper, nor the grubby stuffed animal deities squatting in the closet wall were supposed to exist? Nor the terrycloth bedding with the smell of grandmother's fabric softener? At the end of the film she didn't turn off the TV out of fear. The crackling grey after the programme ended was more comforting than the black night that would have been able to throw her and her narrow room out into space from the eighth floor. Indeed, then she would've been thrown, which would certainly have been worse than falling.

Towards morning, once she had unplugged the TV from the socket next to the bed, she had the feeling that someone else could just as easily pull the plug on her life.

What exactly happens in Part Two? Raoul asks, already in two minds about whether he should come at all next Thursday. Theres Grau pours peanuts into a colourful ceramic bowl.

It goes on like this, says Daniel with his mobile phone in his hand, at least that's what it says online.

Does it get any clearer? Mike asks.

I liked *Matrix* better than this nightmare from the '70s, Theres' boyfriend says. It's simply more modern.

More post-modern, Daniel points out.

That's good, too, Theres' boyfriend adds, but this here is way too slow for me.

Me too, says Mike lounging on a grey sofa, picking at a zit on his chin, looking a bit silly as he continued, in the meantime every child knows ...

What? Theres' boyfriend is quick to ask.

That what is old-fashionedly referred to as the 'I' could basically just be a network of nerve cells in the brain electronically fired around so that it seems like a feeling to us, Mike explains.

But this Stiller, he's sexy, he used to be a dancer before he became an actor. Theres crosses her legs. And anyway, what do you mean 'it's slow'? She bounces a foot until the slipper hits the floor. The film is hardly slower than those that came after, but it's more profound. Besides, a slow pace is also more tender than fast.

Theres stares at her boyfriend. He looks away first. Tim hasn't said anything yet, but tosses a handful of peanuts into his mouth. Alasdair is missing from the film round that Thursday evening, and Theres' boyfriend goes to the toilet for the umpteenth time. Closing the door behind him, he can be heard whistling down the hallway.

That a green tree is just a big pile of molecules, the nightingale's song just an irregular sequence of air pressure fluctuations and the joy of the hiker listening to it only a certain neuronal excitation pattern—not even her professor of neurosurgery had wanted to believe in the end. Man is not only his brain! That is not what the good Lord wants, he had said, after offering her the plate of old ladyfingers in his musty surgery room on the day the Wall fell, a few hours later as ceremoniously as he had offered her the position of assistant doctor.

Do you believe in God, ever heard the name God? What's your name again?

It was shortly before four on that dark afternoon when the professor had tapped his pencil on her CV held still on a green desk pad.

You don't get any federal assistance any more, do you? Why are your studies taking so long?

She opened her mouth to speak.

Because of a man, perhaps? What's his name?

Viktor, she mumbled.

Does he work?

He's an architect and has a job . . .

It's good that he works, the professor said, but don't you want children? I, for example, have six.

She shrugged and looked at the professor's childishly criminal, chronically unbound face that would befit the working title of her doctoral thesis 'Emotional Contagion'—if only she could recall it. That face had so many contradictory features, it stirred alternating mix of feelings in whoever was sat across from it.

Well? Do you believe in God?

God, sure, she replied, looking out the window into a sky of lead. The professor responded, Verily, verily, I tell you, it's 95% certain that God does not exist. But what about the remaining 5%? Well, in the case of His non-existence, both the 5% and the

95% don't matter. But if He does exist, both percentages weigh heavily.

She popped one of the old ladyfingers into her mouth. What had she read in a medical journal the other day about identifying suicidal thoughts in time? It was important to watch out for one's own feelings of emptiness and hopelessness as an indication of similar thoughts in the patient.

The professor's surgery was gloomy, even though it was on the top floor of the clinic. It was musty, even with the windows open. Filled with carved flamingos, two huge accordions by the padded passage door to the secretary, several music stands with manuscripts on them, partly contributions to journals, partly poems, the room did not give the impression of a hospital. Floral dishes lay on the desk, as well as the biscuit plate on a round side table with a rose pattern. Opposite the desk, a picture of Luther and one of Che Guevara hung in identical green frames. But even this combination did not call the professor's professional competence into question. He was simply an elusive person who operated on the open brain with passion. Mostly with success.

Now don't look so sad, he said on the afternoon of 9 November 1989, do you actually know how beautiful a day can be?

I think I do.

Just don't believe too quickly, especially not what the medical books say. Reading the Bible will do. What size gown do you wear?

It's definitely not in the Bible, she'd wanted to reply, but instead said, Thirty-eight.

The professor went to the window and opened it, as if he had noticed the stuffiness of his room. The sun had still been shining in the afternoon, now the sky was closing in, which was hardly noticeable because of the early darkness. Verily, he said, thirty-eight, verily, verily, I thought so. But come your fortieth year, that too will change. For the good Lord wills it so.

That I should grow fatter?

Yes, everything is already written like that in the Bible. Every problem, everything present, everything future and the slipped discs too. Are you familiar with the Old Testament?

No.

You don't know Jacob the Limping Man who wrestles with the angel by the river?

No.

Thought so. In short, the professor looked at her furtively, an angel kicks Jacob, the limping man, on his sciatic nerve at the riverbank. Small act, big effect. Jacob no longer limps. The nerve in the spine, about which it says in the Bible that everyone should enjoy life until the silver cord breaks, this nerve is healed by a single angel's kick. But I, said the professor, I can do that too. Do you know why?

No.

The good Lord wants it that way.

The professor called the morning handover on the ward 'Matutin', 'Matutin' like the first prayer of the day. With the word he bowed to his God. He was an admitted Christian in a team of younger colleagues for whom death was nothing more than the universe's message to the individual that they were not loved, not needed and, actually, did not matter at all. Life on the ward continued after the fall of the Wall as if nothing much had happened. Sometimes in-between the late and early shifts an old man's lower denture would go missing. Sometimes an aneurysm was still being operated at night, although surgeries done after 10 p.m. almost always failed. At the operating table the professor's expression also changed constantly and arbitrarily between joy and fear, between innocence and wickedness, as he spooned altered tissue out of an open brain and refilled the hole with sterile wood and potato starch. The good Lord, He wants it that way, he claimed even as he did so, because actually what he did was bodily harm with possible fatal consequences. Sometimes she had seen animal faces in the foreign tissue during the brain OPs and held on to this uncanny image afterwards, even if a patient called Bobby or Manni could speak as soon as he woke up and say that his name was Bobby and not Robby, or Manni and not Mami, and that he came from England or Eberswalde. Sometimes psalms were sung in the operating theatre when the professor had a particularly successful surgery. The team stuck to the ritual even after a particular patient had heard them singing between light sleeping and deep waking, believed himself to be in heaven and, half-naked and tied to his tubes, had made his escape from the overheated room because he was an atheist, an avowed communist and from the East. When a little intern recaptured him, he could no longer find his way in time, but managed to recite the multiplication table. Of course it's still there, the multiplication table, the professor said, because it's not arithmetic, it's memory. Sometimes a patient wished to die, but their family wouldn't let them. Sometimes there were arguments in the meeting room at second breakfast about the different interpretations of a last will and testament, which could end with an even more heated one about unfair stratification. I also have a right to a life, even if I don't have children, said the new, Chinese assistant doctor taking place of the Hungarian. Besides, I'm going to have a really cool kid one day! Yes, an Asian one, said the ward doctor with the tennis teacher's voice, one that just gets out of the back of the car, runs away in the middle of the crossroads and still grins.

And you, how are you doing at work? Viktor had asked when she had been with the professor for less than a month.

Eating semolina pudding in the canteen and tasting brains, Viktor, why is that?

A reason has many reasons, Viktor had summarized.

He was forty-four and they now lived in an undivided Berlin, a change that was hardly noticeable on Rote Insel in Schöneberg. His teaching job paid well. She had completed her practical year at the hospital and still had a few months ahead of her as an assistant to her professor in neurosurgery.

They had never talked about children.

The river meadows of Havelberg had been behind them. At the end of a bumpy road just before Kremmen, Viktor grabbed her by the shoulder. What a beautiful autumn day, the first without a Wall, he said, but here, through the pines, excavators will soon be rolling in. They will gut the club restaurant over there and tear down the eleven-storey houses, on the other side of the street, along with the colourful corrugated iron balconies. Then no one will live behind the crooked, cardboard windows that are still lit up in the evening, and the area will have become what the West has long since called the Zone. *The Zone*, she repeated. Beneath the word, freezing people crawled out, trying to board a last train that passed between clods of oil and mud to a land that was supposed to be better than the one they fled. A land like a dream.

They were on their foray through Brandenburg that day in a borrowed van. Up until then Viktor had been passionate about flea markets. Ever since the fall of the Wall, the East's refuse became his trove. It was a matter of preserving things that would soon be lost. Sometimes she let herself be infected by his enthusiasm and accompanied him. In general, this man was a contagion for her. He gave her life a surprising sense of meaning, just as Nina had brought colour and warmth in the past. There were dark things too. Still. But they simply didn't talk about them.

If there was nothing put out on the pavements in front of the houses, Viktor was left with the skips from which he could pull his finds. That autumn day he found a purple jewellery box with individually wrapped Meissen lavender soaps, an incomplete moss-green coffee set, a 1973 book on scientific communism, a shopping net made of Dederon, a few colourful plastic egg-carriers in the shape of rushing chickens and a red mug with a broken handle—'Hero of Labour' inscribed on it. As soon as he picked them up, Viktor claimed, the objects started talking to him. The Hero-of-Labour mug told him in its own voice about the day when the handle broke off and rain came. The book on scientific communism knew of a lost world whose guiding principles a reader had painted red and dog-eared for themselves. Viktor read through it the life of a stranger. The newer model Erika typewriter with a dove-blue plastic casing and black keyboard that Viktor had found in front of a doghouse on an earlier expedition—had even dictated a text to him stroke by stroke as he typed, allowing him to make contact with all the people who had ever written on her. When Viktor was out on his own, he only rattled around GDR Berlin on an old cargo bike. In bad weather, he'd put on his dead wife's raincoat. Maybe because the coat felt like an embrace. Or because it was a woman's. Once he had come home with a broken rib because he had leaned too far over the edge of a rain-soaked skip and lost his footing. The rib thing had only happened to me once before, he had said.

When?

While making love, but you were still little then.

He had smiled at her the way one smiles at a strange baby who looks like all the babies in the world. Even like the ones in Ostende.

There, Viktor said, now, stop! Again he grabbed her by her shoulder. They had driven through Kremmen. Just before leaving town, he had spotted two antique school benches under the chestnuts of an empty playground. Solid wood, he exclaimed, with a brightly coated tabletop, and three shelves underneath! A three-seater, probably for chemistry lessons. I love it!

I love you, too, she replied softly, and rounded a bend so sharply that his upper body leant into hers and pressed her against the door.

Careful, Viktor warned, don't veer off like that or we'll end up in a ditch.

They also got the benches. And drove past the river meadows of Havelberg, those scraps of paradise that had settled as a landscape along the shore. An idyll sometimes with, sometimes without sheep. They carried on, Viktor engrossed with the map and hadn't even noticed how on their left, just a moment ago, the riverbank and the water kissed, swallowed each other and then separated again.

Shortly after Kremmen they turned off and took the southern rural road back to Berlin. Lampposts had lit up the villages and they had been less sleepy than those in the West. Sharp and cold, they set their sights on the traffic at their bases.

Daniel is the first to leave. Tim and Mike went after sharing one last drink and arguing about whether they sometimes stink like the lab mice. Whether that's why they always sit alone at the bar, without any women, even though they regularly hit the same club and always shower before. Yes, they both say 'hit'.

She slides off the sofa onto the carpet runner in front of it. She has never done that before. Her body suddenly imitates, involuntarily, the posture of her eighteen-year-old self when she spoke to Viktor on the phone, not that of a thirty-six-year-old when she spoke to Johann. The woman she is now hesitantly begins to trace the loops of the pattern on the carpet with her finger. It would be worth exploring, she thinks, why this move-ment of the fingers on carpet fluff always triggers memories and longing. Tomorrow is Friday and the day after that is Saturday, when at Tegel Airport she wants to announce, Here I am, Mr Storm, as they'd walk towards each other, and maybe he would yawn wearily thanks to his last nightcap with Sergei or because of the women in provocatively well-trimmed schoolgirl uni-forms waitressing at the bar.

She pours herself more wine and reclines on the sofa.

After her boyfriend has gone to bed, Theres begins to talk. About the beginning of her studies, about her first night in the dormitory and about a young woman with frizzy hair who was standing next to her bed at around three in the morning, in the light of a streetlamp that lit the room. With the flickering of the room lamp, the woman disappeared, Theres recounts, but hesitates . . .

Theres is beautiful when she hesitates, she thinks.

. . . but the room was sad afterwards, you see?

She nods.

Next morning, I described the incident to the people in the administration. 'Fits,' the lettings woman said, 'must have been your predecessor. She took her own life at the end of last month, in that room.' You get it?

Again she nods. In her head, noisy little birds are flying together over an empty space.

You see, you understand it all. Why did someone like you become a scientist?

What should she say now?

Theres pours more wine.

Did the visitor ever come back, Theres?

No.

And if she had, what would you have done?

I would have lifted her eyelid to see if her pupil was fixed, immobile and unrounded, then I would have poured ice water into her ear and, finally, I would have seen if the gag reflexes would stop when I fiddled with the back of her throat with a gloved finger.

You wouldn't have.

Yes, I would.

No way.

Yes, I would have just checked the facts of death, believe me! Theres squealed.

And where would you have got ice water and gloves so quickly?

Well, what would you have done, huh? Prayed? Theres got up and said, I thought you knew about dark things. I thought you understood me. You've been dead before.

I think I have to go now.

Just because you were dead once?

Theres walks up to the door but stops without turning around. Look carefully, she whispers, barely audible. This is Theres, says Theres, a person everyone thinks they know. She is Baltic blonde, an ambitious researcher, seen from the front. From the back, however, she's still Baltic blonde, but is also a seer of spirits with a Slavic grandmother. Do you see it that way too?

Still better than a lyceum from the back and a museum from the front, she replies, with the taste of artificial honey in her mouth.

Theres turns around, and asks: Is this a saying of yours?

No, my grandmother's.

Well, give my regards to this grandmother of yours. I'd like to meet her.

Long dead, she replies. And you, by the way, shouldn't think too much about death.

Why not?

Because you don't have any children yet.

Theres turns back to the door to switch on the overhead light.

On the table is a lighter that Mike must have forgotten. If she uses it now, its clack-clack will remind her of another Zippo, once the tuning fork of a perfect afternoon on the bonnet of an old, now ancient, white Mercedes long ago. When Johann dies, I wonder if anyone will let her know . . .

Your boyfriend, how old is he, Theres? she asks.

How old do you think he is?

Thirty-six?

Theres shrugs. Wrong, seven, she answers, as old as all men. After that point, he's simply grown physically.

A few minutes later she is standing in the drizzle on the quiet street in front of the little end rowhouse where Theres lives with her boyfriend. The *wah-wah* of a trumpet from an old film accompanies her through the night as she walks to the bus. Here I am, she says to the driver as she gets on, and realizes that she is no longer sober. The heels of her shoes are higher than they were a moment ago, and the damp coat collar melts like rhubarb leaf over her shoulders, as if she were no longer herself, but an actress from the '50s with a big tragic mouth who wants to take a bus from the Berlin public utility company to a man who is ten thousand kilometres away in Siberia.

*Wah-wah* . . . All that's missing are the lace gloves.

She sits behind the bus driver.

Hey, hey, Johann had repeated too often that Saturday. Cloth in hand, he wiped a puddle of tea from the designer table in the kitchen. The silver espresso machine was on the cooker. Something about horror films he had been talking about while the coffee rose in the moka pot. Then he sat down. At Nina's table. He, a cleaner hired by Nina. She felt sorry for him and slid her arms across the top until its edge bumped into her armpits. Hey now, don't worry, Beautiful, she won't be back in twenty minutes either. She won't come back as long as we're both here, Johann had said, getting up again, reaching out to the strange-looking fridge for a bottle of beer which he opened with a disposable lighter.

He seemed to have forgotten the espresso.

Your Johann is a good man, her grandmother would have said, he drinks but doesn't hurt you. Yes, Johann was a good man. With his drinking, he only hurt himself.

I never asked you if you had anything together? she said.

No answer.

Tell me, did you have something together?

Who?

Nina and you, back when we met on New Year's Eve at your milk action in the tram just past Hackescher Markt?

Why?

The winters in Berlin are cold, opportunity makes love, one reason has many reasons . . . and so on.

Johann looked at her sullenly. Behind this displeasure, it was becoming increasingly difficult to discover once again the beautiful melancholy that had charmed her from the beginning.

Did you?

What now? his tone was alarming, I've got enough strength till right here, right here, Beautiful.

Did you sleep with each other or not?

All right, Johann said, once, and only briefly.

Two hours later, they had finished cleaning. The last thing she did was to cover the two down blankets on the king-sized bed with fresh synthetic linen. Then she washed her hands in the bathroom and opened the patchouli bottle in front of the mirror. She took a drop and rubbed it into her neck. Let's go! Johann called from the hallway, Time to leave, Beautiful, it's already past two. When she came out of the bathroom, he was standing there with the cleaning supplies. Tenderly he stroked her bare shoulder and adjusted the strap of the man's shirt. He smelt her.

Is that new?

On the Biedermeier dresser next to the bouquet of orchids lay a small banknote.

A tip, she said, a tip from Nina. She pocketed it.

In the evening they ate spaghetti bolognese on the balcony. As on every clear night, a pale but now full moon wandered millimetre by millimetre along the gap between the roofs. She reached for it and held it briefly between her thumb and forefinger. What are you doing? Johann asked but didn't wait for the answer. He carried the plates inside. Four summers ago, on his fortieth birthday, he had drunkenly hurled the chestnut from the balcony into the courtyard and said quietly, fuck-you-fuck-you, I don't want a child. He clenched his hand in a fist for a moment, and went on to get a beer. I don't want one from you either, she had muttered behind him, thinking about Viktor, how he had behaved on his fortieth birthday. How, actually? She didn't remember. Why not? She held her breath. Then the familiar anxiety began to grow. She had almost forgotten it. The frightful feeling. And the man, too. Shit, she thought, I've become what I've forgotten, haven't I? But I'm not the only one.

Again she reached for the moon. Again she held the disc between her thumb and forefinger and tried to push it back along its path. But nothing could turned back, anti-clockwise. But I'm not the only one, I'm not the only one who has to live with this feeling, she repeated. Was that any consolation? The moon just kept on wandering while the opened letter she had taken out of the box that afternoon still lay on the kitchen table. An institute for clinical neurobiology in Berlin had offered her a job as an additional project manager for the laboratory with some office duties from the beginning of next year. She would probably end up something like a slightly better-off secretary, but it was a permanent position.

She hadn't told Johann about her job interview—she'd gone one morning and returned the same evening. She'd walked along the Rhine alone that evening, thinking about Berlin. The river had seemed so beautiful to her. So beautiful, with a hint of a possible farewell. How ugly the Spree was in comparison. But the move to Berlin wouldn't work out anyway, she had thought. She was forty-four, had never made a name for herself at work and no longer believed herself to be any good. Besides, she liked being in the flat they shared at the Wehrhahn. There, at the end of the day, she had a Johann. He, like her, a sad forty-four. Suddenly she liked their small, if precarious, life together again. It was that kind of feeling, just a feeling, she realized, and then it was over, the feeling. Suppose she had told Johann about the job in Berlin and asked, Are you coming with me? He would have just stood there, saying nothing, and in doing so would already have failed. I hate to see you like this, Johann, she had muttered, watching a barge on its way to Holland. Tomorrow's another day, you would now object, Johann, but not a better one. The times when I would say, If you leave me one day, I'll come with you, are over. And if I leave now, will you follow me? You'll have to work up the momentum for that on your own, my dear Johann, you know I don't have any reserves left for two. The two of us have pressed helplessly against each other for too long, and watched the old balloon of our love run out of air.

The letter was on the kitchen table. The rag they had used to wipe Nina's flat was hanging over the balcony parapet. Above it, the moon continued to wander. She sat down on the stool where the sweet chestnut had once lived. Johann followed from the kitchen with a beer which wasn't even cold from the case next to the door. When he went to open it, the lighter fell. He crouched down to pick it up, and when he put the lighter back against the cap of the bottle, it slipped again. This time it fell at her feet. She didn't move, but said, I can't go on, sometimes I can't go on either . . . Johann remained still, crouching, not looking up at her. I'm going to Berlin, she declared.

She did not ask, Are you coming with me?

Was there such a thing as a lumbago in the heart? She drew her knees up to her belly, and he got down slowly on all fours, as if in answer. Then he pushed his head forward a little to press his forehead against her shins. And so they remained, mistress and dog, both tense in a relatedness that had become obsolete.

No, they never got married.

She went to Berlin. He stayed on the Rhine. They separated spatially, then irreconcilably.

**31.8**

What a beautiful dress, says Volvo Man. Soon it will be autumn. That's why my wool dress is the colour of a colourful salad and with a narrow stripe at the cuff and the hem. Poppy colours.

**2.9**

I hear footsteps in the flat above me, then in my own. A small dog runs past. Then a man. A burglar. Before the burglar disappears from my dream, he calls out: My name is Russian.

**13.9**

Everything, everything comes from the past, from when you were a child.

**14.9**

Sort the shelves. Everything's a mess.

Pavese/*The Devil in the Hills*, Radiguet/*The Devil in the Flesh*, Aragon/*The Lilacs and the Roses*, Susan Sontag/*Where the Stress Falls*.

I crack open Alexander Kluge: For people, *curricula vitae* become houses whenever crisis reigns outside.

I highlighted that. When? Or rather: Why?

FRIDAY

00.37 on Friday morning. A silhouette on the first floor of No. 7 Schenkendorfstraße, Berlin Kreuzberg, near the market hall and Trinity Cemetery. The curtain to the street is thin. On the pavement in front of the house is a brownish carpet. No foliage, just dead blossoms from the linden trees along the street. Isn't that sick, coming here at night with the bus and the *wah-wah* of a Miles Davis trumpet in my head to call a strange man on a landline so that my ringing is present for a moment in his flat, and I'll hear it all the way out into the street? A way to be connected without really being connected.

Hello, who's speaking?

It's me, she almost answered the woman's voice, I just don't know right now if I'm fourteen or fifty-four, and if I don't have roof damage like any old barn that burns to the ground once it's in love. It's me, the woman from the airport, who drinks her little pilsner there on weekends, sometimes two, and then secretly pulls business cards out of younger men's wallets to take as tokens of love even though they're only stolen. Yes, I'm just the same as I used to be—walking beside Nina in a faux-fur hat, white patent boots and in love, in front of the English teacher's house before finding out he's gay. Yes, that's who I still am, the inconspicuous one, but the one who would surely be criminalized or psychiatrized if anyone took a closer look. The one who would perhaps have been better off as a roofer instead of a brain researcher . . .

Her ear is laughing now, or is she just imagining that too?

Earlier, while getting on the bus, she'd showed the driver one of the many stamped tickets she'd already used to travel out to Tegel or to Schenkendorfstraße on Monday. The driver glanced at her face, not at the stamp on the ticket. Thanks, he said. Not for that, she replied. Has she always been crazy, or just too brash for a moment?

Hello, still there? At her ear there is actually a laugh, friendly, warm. She looks up to the first floor of No. 7 Schenkendorfstraße. Two windows are lit. All the others are hung with sheets of darkness. Does the building have a lift? A lift to the scaffold, *wah-wah*, and how crazy is it to come here anyway? The ringing of a telephone up there won't conjure the man she wants to talk to without having anything to say to him. It only makes the woman who picked up the phone in the middle of the night uneasy. His wife. Now she may suspect that there's another woman. *Wah-wah*, yes how silly that is, but how pleasant it feels not to be alone in the night but to be part of a triangle.

Hello?

The silhouette on the first floor has stepped closer to the bright curtain and is holding her head tilted to the side, looking patiently or empathetically. The woman at the window, whose name may be Stein, is putting something in her mouth. Chocolate, perhaps? From down here she's too fat, and now that she turns briefly to the side, she clearly has a belly.

Hello, still there? Suppressed call? Come on, talk to me . . .

Why doesn't the woman just hang up? Does she like anonymous calls? Are they not a threat, but rather a promise that life could behave according to the rules of a novel from now on and pick up speed? I'm going to get myself a gun, dear Robert, the woman at the window may call out on Saturday to greet him, barely having entered the flat in No. 7. I'm going to shoot this other woman, Robert! If the target ends up only being in my imagination, in the end nobody dies, dearest, and I'd just shoot into the air. But me, I'll feel better afterwards . . .

Coming over here Kreuzberg seemed to be in a deep sleep, like a secluded village in winter snow. Only the outlines of an osteria's lettering right next door were visible, hollow without any light. A balmy air and a strange silence surrounded them. Not the slightest sign of life from another human being indicated that she was not alone in the world. She'd got off the bus at Trinity Cemetery for the second time in a week, as if there to visit the grave of a recently deceased dear one. But the gate to the cemetery was locked. Cemeteries always lock up at dusk, of course. Still, she was on the lookout for a man in white trousers who might be Viktor, or maybe just his revenant, waiting there for her with a rusty key, a bottle of vodka and two Russian standard-sized glasses so that after seventy minutes of touring the cemetery with him she would realize: That's how it is, stories always end with a child or with death, cheers!

But no one had been standing in front of the gate. Only in front of the market hall diagonally opposite, where the furniture had remained chained outside for the night, an overweight woman sat with her bags crammed into one of the chairs. She slept, making the night larger.

Come on, talk to me, sweetheart, the voice in her ear says now.

What do you mean sweetheart?!

She slaps her hand over her mouth to keep from answering out loud. A taxi turns in at the beginning of the street and drives towards No. 7. It is an old white Mercedes. I didn't know they still existed. It pulls to the side of the road a few steps away, in front of the osteria, and cuts its headlights. No one gets out.

I know that the Stasi or the Nazis are watching you again, dear, the voice in her ear says. I know that the car is just pretending to be from Telekom, and it's parked right in front of your door, just like in the good old days. Just like before reunification . . .

Is she, the woman up there at the window, in fact tired? Or is her voice always so lascivious, even when saying ridiculous things?

. . . and the man who briefly got out of the suspicious car this morning and stepped onto the street has tapped your phone, sweetheart, I know. He's listening in right now too, from his car. I also know what you want to say now—just because you're paranoid doesn't mean you're not being followed. But you and I discussed all these circumstances earlier this afternoon. Apparently, even now, in the middle of the night, you have no new information to add to your reproachful silence. It's really late. Take your diazepam now, you hear me? I know it's the last one, you said so earlier this afternoon. Tomorrow we'll get you a new prescription from your doctor, and now, good night, Mom.

Mom?!

A little squeak answers. The woman at the window, however, has not choked, but hung up. Not even the soft murmur of a mild steady rain remains in the phone as before.

She looks up at the first floor of No. 7 Schenkendorfstraße. The curtain is thin and white, but it is not an answer. The woman is still standing behind the curtain. For a moment, the flat and the street are the same waiting hall. Then the woman disappears into the depths of the room. The light on the second floor goes out. Now the house is completely dark. Only she, down on the brown carpet of dead linden blossoms, is still there—an old, empty barn by the wayside, the harvests long gone. But wait, linden blossoms in August? Did she get the month wrong? Or is she lost in time?

Excuse me.

She turns around.

Excuse me, miss.

A man had got out of the white Mercedes and was sitting on the bonnet. If he lights a cigarette with the click of a Zippo, she'll know for sure that someone is playing a nasty trick on her. Someone has deliberately misconnected some wires in her head, and that man over there isn't real and neither is anything around him or her. Which proves once again that reality doesn't really exist.

She crosses her arms in front of her chest, walks up to the man and asks, Do you have a cigarette?

How brusque that sounded.

Sorry, the man replies, I don't smoke any more, but did you order a cab?

Almost seven hours later, it's 8 a.m. on a Friday. Her boss picked up her mice at dawn to fly to Washington. Surely there are also a few of the depressed animals that always remain sitting in the back left corner of the cage after the experiments. 'Rhythm of the Brain' that's what her boss will talk to her American colleagues about. She likes to fly to the States. My old home, she says. Before leaving she must have been in the office. She put a newspaper article on her colleague's desk and highlighted a section in yellow. For a life, it says, is determined —more than one would like to believe—by what is missing. By the paths that have not been taken. And one will always entertain notions of a better life in a better place with an even better person. This is not a bad thing, so long as we build a home for ourselves that is good enough and this unlived life does not gain too much power over us. Besides, much more often than we think, we are already precisely where we need to be . . .

Next to the article there's a handwritten note: For Konstanze. Could you please finally hang the three pictures? Thank you!

Next to it lies the hammer.

Johann had taught her how to use tools such as spirit levels, drills, nails and hammers. Viktor had taught her to eat spaghetti with a fork (no spoon) and Asian food with chopsticks. He had shown her how to recognize and distinguish between epochs of buildings and paintings, or how to listen intently at the opera, even when there are giant seats blocking the view of the stage. Johann had shown her how nice it can be to be faithful and to have a home, after Viktor had shown her how to cheat and let one cheat. A certain Rüdiger, who was listed in Viktor's calendar as an evening date every week, had turned out to be named Almut. She herself had had affairs and forgotten about Viktor's roll-top cabinet. But where were your memories when you weren't having them?

What we have forgotten has become what we are. Who had said that again, is so long ago? The friend who was so good at laying needlefelt after he stopped studying sports and started studying critical psychology? Unlikely. In preparation for his new studies, he had read *Das Kapital* and jotted down key sentences on index cards. Before his exams, she had eavesdropped on him. *Art is not a mirror to reflect reality, but a hammer with which to shape it.* She remembered that sentence. Viktor had had his own opinion about the hammer and sickle. For him, they were not tools, but symbols of the unity of the working and peasant class, even after the end of the GDR. In his opinion, communism was supposed to have happened long before reunification. According to the plan of the People's Chamber, the West was to have been surpassed by 1961, including in economic terms, socialism was to have been achieved in 1965, and communism was to have been installed between 1980 and 2000, although the feasibility of all these plans had already been proven by Sputnik in 1957, when it surpassed the old world in space. Disintegration of an old space, Viktor had added. Viktor would probably still be searching for the whereabouts of all those ideas today, at night, standing at the window and looking down at the streetlamps, which awakened a feeling of loneliness in him, until he too went to sleep, curled up in a red flag.

And Johann?

She takes the hammer from the desk. It weighs heavily in her hand. Where is the man who will teach her how to live happily up through the end?

Whoever laughs at fairy tales, was never in distress, Viktor had said when she asked why he actually made these shoebox-sized worlds. They had already been together for thirteen years. He worked on his fairy-tale scenarios in the flat across the hall like a set designer designing spaces for political theatre productions that would change the world. Sometimes she would look up from her doctoral dissertation, 'Emotional Contagion', and see him over at the table pondering, tinkering, gluing. Sometimes he would hold up a model for her in the window and she would nod from across the courtyard. Then, sometimes, she was overcome by desolation at the thought that this working alone yet as a couple, the silence and the words they shared in the evening, their winters and summers and themselves too, sooner or later would be over. But whether this was her mood or Viktor's, she could not have said. The long-distance relationship had become one at a short distance. She was also able to observe how Viktor would leave without her from the side-wing flat across the courtyard and only come back at night. And when she went over to sleep with him in the back room she could see how his eyes shined, a glow beneath his pale skin. There, besides the bed, the green-tiled stove, the roll-top cabinet—but locked up tight—and some suitcases which had remained as unpacked as Viktor's down blankets unventilated. By the time she had arrived at the chapter 'Neurophysiology of Facial Expressions', she bought herself her first computer.

In one of Viktor's dioramas 'Gretchen Dutschke in a Wedding Dress' had got lost in a hilly area of hay and straw at the hand of a Hansel whose oversized face wore an Adorno mask. A signpost tree, pasted inside according to the rules of the golden section, offered the couple half a dozen destinations. Wiesengrund, Passage B, concentration camp, car park, Hollywood, childhood, table and bed, incinerator, cemetery, marquee. There was no distance marked on any of the tiny signs, only the direction. A direction that seemed a bit vague to her. She was in her early thirties and Viktor was eighteen years older, nothing had changed. He had, however, become smaller. Sometimes his mouth smelt like books and often she had difficulty understanding him. That wasn't good, that wasn't bad. It was the way it was. And had she ever understood him, this older man who had once been an angry student, kicking down the doors in the administration hallway of Freie Universität in the summer of '68 after a man named Teufel proclaimed himself rector?

Pretty stupid, that action, she said as he was telling her about the battles of the extra-parliamentary opposition times over coffee one day.

We were radical, but not stupid.

Viktor had replied with a tug around his mouth that said he still felt indebted to the cultural revolutionary movements of the century. Lukács, Adorno, Horkheimer, Marcuse, Bloch, Reich and, of course, Dutschke and Marx. On one of his shelves where the books were crowded into two rows there was an old photograph of him, showing a Viktor with a look of dismay, a childlike melancholy. The person taking the picture had probably asked him to be funny. Now Viktor sometimes looked at her that way, even though she never took pictures.

Did you have anything to do with the RAF, Viktor?

You mean with Hans and Grete?

Who are Hans and Grete?

Code names for Baader and Ensslin, so tell me, who's actually the stupid one here?

OK, she said, but the line about the fairy tales, you stole that?

And if I did? Viktor had said, it wouldn't make it any less true.

Shall we? Viktor asked in early March when the brothel in the front building closed down.

One Saturday two drivers were loading the last of the wall mirrors into a truck from Poland as she went out to go shopping for breakfast around nine. One was Viktor's age and short of breath. The other, tattooed all the way over the backs of his hands and about her age, was obviously on speed and helping the older one out. When she returned a little later, the tattooed man paused on the pavement. He eyed her, the woman with a bag of rolls and a newspaper, and when he smiled, she saw that he was shy.

A few minutes later, as she was making coffee in his tiny kitchen, Viktor said loudly from the next room, Yes, we should!

What?

Move into the front building.

That evening the building owner removed the 'Club Sophie' and 'The Business' signs from the doorbell. He stuck copies of the signs 'FOR RENT WITHOUT COMMISSION' on the windows facing the street. On Tuesday, Viktor signed the contract. He wanted to leave the dark non-woven wallpaper on the walls of the five narrow rooms as well as the oxblood-red painted floorboards in the hallway.

Original, he thought.

Creepy, she said.

Two beds still stood in the last room where two old double windows looked out onto the courtyard. They were tall and narrow, with handles at the head ends.

Could be pushed together for comfort, Viktor said.

Could just as well not, she said, and was glad that at least the heavy, dark curtains to the street had disappeared when they were cleared out, even if the sight of cars inching past the bare windows a perceived arm's length away in rain-soaked tracks wasn't all that comforting.

At Ikea they bought a kitchen and new toilet lids for the two bathrooms and argued over the appropriate colours—a fact that reassured her. They were a normal couple after all. When the owner of the house handed the bunch of keys to Viktor, she recognized the tag with the words 'Coal Cellar' on one of them. She had written that herself once. Ever since the cubbyhole down there became a *business*, the building owner said, holding her gaze, there's been an intercom and a security door, but no more coal or potatoes. Still, many thanks, beautiful woman, may this be a memory of your youth. He had a strong, calm, sarcastic face. How carefree and confidently he spoke. How old could he be? Younger than Viktor, obviously. The building owner took the key from the ring and pressed it into her hand. In the collar of his white shirt she saw the flash of a gold necklace. His fingers, closing over hers, were a vise.

The old wooden shed had been torn down, the new plaster wall to the hallway painted anthracite grey, and the former coal cellar merged with two adjacent rooms. Next to the low security door stood forlorn a bucket of potatoes from which thin white sprouts had sprung up. Weren't these pale fingers that grew in the dark known as fear shoots? She unlocked the door and was startled by the spotlights that flared up as soon as she pushed the door open with her foot. Islands of shadow and light spread across black shelves, glass cases, ropes on the walls, and plucked at a gynaecological chair from a corner. Someone had put long wigs over the stirrups. In front of it was a cage that would have been big enough for a lion complete with mane, next to it a gym rack with a handful of whips on the leather covering, their number doubled in a large wall mirror. Behind the door an open moving box with a rubber penis shaped like a carrot and several gas masks awaited removal. The walls were soundproofed with red foam rubber, and a boombox sat on a metal bed in the centre of the room. When she pressed the button, a march played. Mixed in with the music was a human voice.

This is a Transylvanian military march . . .

It was Viktor's voice. Before she could turn around, a potato flew sharply past her ear and sprang onto the metal bed. The laughter that followed sounded like the call of a peacock. It had been just like that before. Exactly the same! Even if I forget everything else here, she had thought at the time, I will never forget this laughter, even if I become senile. Only now did she turn to the voice. Viktor was playing with a second potato, tossing it into the air like a juggler and catching it again as he walked towards the metal bed to sit on the latex coverlet. Oh, that's Viktor, she thought as she looked over at him, eyes widening. That's Viktor—not someone who loves me, but someone who observes. She stared at him, unblinking. Yes, that was Viktor, all of it—the rack and the whip, the rubber penis and the wigs.

What is it, what's wrong, why are you looking at me as if I want to poison you? Viktor asked, reaching for the boom box.

I want to sit down, too, she said with a croak in her voice, as if the poison had already taken effect. With one hand, she cleared a small chair that stood in the shadow of the gynaecological chair. I'll just sit here and concentrate for a moment, she decided, but suddenly laughed. You know what I was just thinking about, Viktor? she said. About how I heard the words 'concentration camp' for the first time and thought, That's where I'll end up if I don't learn to concentrate . . .

Viktor turned off the music. How embarrassing that was now, to hear one's own breathing. Come here, Viktor said from the bed, tapping the seat next to him.

What a nightmare. She stopped next to the little chair. After more than thirty years, this life had not become her life. It might as well be someone else's, and if she was going to lose it soon, it hadn't been good for anything better than loss.

It's cute, this little one, she heard herself say in her rusty voice, before slowly getting down on her knees to sit down.

That's not a child's chair, by the way, Viktor said, it's the slave's.

On the last weekend in March, Viktor and she moved into the five dark rooms, front building, ground floor. Viktor paid the rent. From her work desk she now no longer watched the second floor in the side wing. Nevertheless, she made little progress with her doctoral thesis. Perplexed, or dull from thinking about emotional contagion, one afternoon she turned on the small TV next to the table, where a gleefully pubescent Britney Spears was hosting the *Mickey Mouse Club*. Emotional contagion, she realized then, was a simple thing. In the presence of a happy Britney, everyone felt happy, but around a sad person such as herself, everyone became sad or, at the very least, annoyed. She turned off the TV and opened Chapter Five entitled 'Interaction between Perception and Production of Facial Expressions'. Why did she actually find it so difficult to reasonably describe the chosen methodology, to put the investigated symptoms into language and to cram them into tables at the end of each chapter in a result-oriented way? She turned the TV back on. The young Britney, bouncing around the stage singing in her printed shirt and dancing aerobic, sounded like a grown woman. It was possible that one day she would pay a heavy price for this mistimed mimicry and made to sound like a little girl as an adult. Whatever. She turned up the volume and bounced along.

For a short time, she felt better.

For months, men still came by asking about Club Sophie or The Business in the cellar, even though neither was on the doorbell any more. Most customers were looking for a certain Java with a tattoo of a scorpion on her left hand. But it was the eyes that were beguiling, raved a wizened but well-dressed gentleman late one evening, whom she had already seen driving up in a taxi from the kitchen window. She was alone in the flat. Leaning into the frame of the door to the landing, she folded her arms over the belt of her bathrobe. I'm actually a wine merchant, the withered gentleman said, may I come in for a moment? Such an old man and still at it? Goethe, Viktor had said the other day, had sex for the first time at thirty-six. And when was the last time? she'd asked.

May I? the withered gentleman repeated. Turmoil on his face. For a brief moment, a sadness that had inscribed itself around his mouth and eyes over the decades gave way to a different feeling. The trace of lust tore through his thin, aged skin.

May I? he repeated.

No, she smiled teasingly.

Viktor kept his small flat in the side wing as an office and library. She rented hers to a young man from Leipzig who was studying theology and economics. His father was from the Middle East, his mother from Saxony. The young man became her personal fire brigade, coming over to help whenever the new computer stopped working. After that, he liked to stay for a while. She listened to his flaming speeches over a beer. As a student he had been involved with Hope for Nicaragua in the GDR. Once upon a time in Nicaragua, she said one evening, plopping on the sofa but keeping her feet on the ground. Viktor wasn't home. The young man from Leipzig threw himself next to her. He smelt very different from Viktor. Of fresh wood. It made her think of Rome, of the sea near Ostia, where years ago an old woman had walked along the beach past Viktor and her. With a wooden bucket on her back, she had counted: *uno, due, tre.* The old man next to her had howled like a wolf and the grandson at his hand kept on walking. What a clever boy, she'd thought, he knew as long as you have the sea, you don't lack anything. Not even longing . . .

By the time she and the young man from Leipzig stopped kissing, it had almost become dark outside. A child in the court-yard was singing the word 'Mama' as a scale. Fits, she thought. Once we move out of here, Viktor and I, this flat will probably become a day-care centre. Nothing is just what it is, nor is it the way it stays.

Then Viktor showed up with a suggestion. He had brought— as if to give her courage—a poem as an epilogue for her PhD thesis.

It is nonsense
says reason
It is what it is
says love

It is unhappiness
says calculation
It is nothing but pain
says fear
It is hopeless

says insight
It is what it is
says love

It is ridiculous
says pride
It is foolish
says caution
It is impossible
says experience
It is what it is
says love.


Was the poem a declaration of love?

Thank you, Viktor, she said.

It's nothing. It is what it is, he said, holding her wrist and gently turning it until the palm looked up as if begging. There are poetic truths to be discovered in the sciences, Viktor said, mouth on her pulse, before kissing the strands of veins beneath the thin skin. He kisses my soul, she thought. There it was again, that shiver he called *frisson érotique*. Simply saying gooseflesh was not poetic enough for someone like Viktor.

For what good is a science that is of no use to the metaphysics of this world? said Viktor.

Agreed, she said.

He reached for her other wrist and looked at the watch.

Over the following weeks a certain magic dwelt in her writing about emotional contagion. Whenever he went out, at her table she became a traveller in facial features. Became a feverish researcher in the field of mimicry. In her last chapter on 'Arbitrary Mimicry and Humour' she listed emotional reactions of subjects to funny cartoons. Even cheerfulness could be expressed in percentages. She enjoyed working on this last chapter, and rearranged the photos of laughing or smiling women between the tables over and over again.

A small poem with a big impact, says Love?

Winter came more quickly than expected but brought little snow. Winter, said Viktor, is the true season of the soul. The beautiful acacias to the right and left on the pavement in front of the building had already lost not only their leaves in September—the bark lay like the crusts of wounds. Viktor raised his moist finger in the air like a boy scout. Ever since the Wall fell, there's a draught, he said, the trees notice it too.

She was making good progress on her thesis, even with the proofreading, and was looking forward to the day when she would take a fat stack of text to the copy store and choose the colour of the cover page.

The joy was shortlived.

Viktor went on a trip. To Moscow, he said in a tone as if he no longer fathomed life without Moscow. As he packed his hard-side suitcase—which he'd hunched over and dragged behind him on noisy rollers on their vacations together—she stood beside it as if on the edge of a fire where she was freezing.

Pass me my underwear, please, a fresh pair for each day. You never know what kind of situation you'll get into.

Viktor smiled, surprising her with how handsome he still was after all these years. He was no longer young, but there still was a spirit of adventure about him.

Are you still a communist, Viktor?

What does that have to do with underwear?

She walked to the bathroom and saw in the mirror the hair-thin lines around her lips, which became more and more like imprints of bird claws in the sand. The feeling named Ostende had left its mark.

From Moscow Viktor brought back a scar on his head, which had been well stitched there in the hospital, she noted with the doctor's gaze. One night on his way home to the hotel, he said, he had run into a police raid and, being a West Berliner teddy-bear, as he good-humouredly called himself, had realized too late that the men's uniforms were fake, and that the officers in them were criminals with wooden slats in their jacket sleeves. They beat him indiscriminately when he didn't hand over his money. The lady attendant on the eighteenth floor of his Hotel Moskva had not been a fat, old woman crocheting lace doilies next to the elevator, but an Irina who drew. She drove him to the nearest outpatient clinic on a motorcycle.

Irina. Just hearing the name made her sulk.

Six months later, Irina moved into the side wing with Viktor's books. Between her hometown in Central Asia, where the steppes were shamelessly covered with carpets of poppies in May, and a greyish Ostende that smelt like fish halls, lay two days of travel by train. For her, however, this Irina came from Ostende. Not in reality, but in truth, even if this woman said she was born in Kazakhstan. There was a wild abandon to Irina's eyes, but also that certain look that men think is devotion, but women think cunning. Her curls were the colour of fire. Irina smelt good, like fruit and tobacco, and now sat at the window where once the mother and daughter from Siberia had eaten polenta or sour-cream cake. She painted the tree in the court-yard, the view of the sky or the view of the flat in the opposite side wing. With a few strokes there sat a knitting woman at the window.

How can this Russian woman know what was once reflected in my windows, Viktor?

She doesn't, he replied, but what she doesn't, she makes up.

Irina was often very hungry.

After a few weeks, Irina got a place to study stage design and costume at the academy of fine arts. A friend of Viktor's had written a letter of confirmation for the visa that she would work at the Berliner Ensemble as an assistant stage designer. In her first semester, she made a bedstead out of tree cuttings and bark that she had found on the street in front of the building after a violent storm. The mattress, however, was black, peaty soil from the supermarket on which she sowed wildflowers. As if infected by her project, Viktor devoted himself with renewed energy to his fairy-tale scenarios. Once, as he was kicking a stone in front of him in the courtyard before disappearing into the side wing with his lodger, she would have loved to shout after them: Hey, what are you doing, you going to fuck now?! Small, shabby and as mean as the word made her feel at that moment. But it nested in her head and became a stupid counting rhyme.

Knit, kick, fuck.

If she knew Irina was alone in the work flat, she felt like ringing the bell and storming past a baffled, wild-eyed deer-face, into Viktor's back room, grabbing the superglue from the table, while knocking Viktor's silly models over, unscrewing the glue, shoving its tip into the lock of the roll-top cabinet and squeezing it shut. Be glad I'm doing this! Be glad, with all that pornographic junk in there! she would shout, and then throw the glue behind her onto the grey felt floor with a grand gesture, as if it were a burning match that would torch any residual agreements that might still apply to Viktor and her. Sometimes, however, in her imagination she would approach Irina's nose with the tube open and ask, Well, what does that smell like to you? Like birch? Do you love birch trees? Then go back to where they grow, you Russian. At the latest then, she was sure, Irina would turn from a stunned into an aggressive deer and scream: I can kick, bite and scratch. Get lost, you nothing, you were only someone before you were born!

The idea of fighting Irina filled her with satisfaction.

Soon after, she got colic. As if someone had poisoned her. Was it Irina? Viktor? Or she herself? The doctor she went to see said that the signs of death first appear behind the ears and on the ankles. As a doctor, she knew it too. But that this fact could have something to do with her made the little fright that had been sitting inside her for a long time grow. The doctor asked her to take off her shoes and stockings and pinched the thin skin over her Achilles tendon. The jumper under his gown was the same colour as his hair. Rust.

Were you an overachiever at school? Did you always do everything right, but without feeling? Do you ever grope about within your own emptiness?

He massaged the narrow bridge above the heel.

Be careful that this doesn't aggravate, he said. You can fret about it for another three weeks. But that's it.

For two weeks she lay on one of the two high, narrow beds in the back room, even during the day. Where the handles had once been screwed on at the head end, two black holes peered out of the wall like tiny skylights. One she called space, the other time. It is unhappiness, they answered one day. It is nothing but pain, they said, already more fearful, the following day.

It is ridiculous, a residue of pride rebuked her.

It was what it was.

In the third week she moved in with Nina. The man named Johann did not exist for either of them at the time. Nina wanted to go abroad for a long time with a theatre collective. Or maybe just to the Rhineland, she added with a laugh, and left her the keys to the flat. They still knew each other well, but their friendship had suffered because of Viktor. No, Viktor wasn't jealous, but he was very particular and preferred seclusion. Sometimes with him, she felt as if she had even forgotten the language of the country they lived in. As if she no longer needed to learn it either. Talking to Viktor was enough. Sometimes she also felt as if she lived in wild abandon with him in a lonely, small, black garden house, through the cracks of which they saw the sky together.

Nina's street had beautiful acacias out in front, too, just like the building where she had lived with Viktor. She would have liked Nina, her friend, to share the flat with her. To have her working in the kitchen behind a half-open door, opening a biscuit tin for the both of them with a metallic sigh, pouring water or setting an egg timer to steep tea for two. How she liked such sounds. Someone was there, not quite close, but taking care of her.

But at Nina's too she lay on the bed and slowly began to wilt. Like the women in Russian literature, she thought angrily. At night, a large moon wandered along in the window, making the stars appear thinner. Something at the bottom of her mind was a passing memory or foreboding that wanted to skim to the top, but would be better off otherwise, and that hurt like heartbreak. She remembered that, one night, when Viktor and she still lived hundreds of kilometres apart, in a fit of love she had said on the phone, When you're dead, Viktor, I'm going to put a bench on your grave. Why would you do that? he had asked And she had replied: So I can sit there and eat my loaf of bread when I come to visit you, and if I leave some crumbs behind, the birds will have some, too, before they fly off again.

But I don't want a bench on my grave, Viktor had protested.

Why not?

Imagine a bench that's always empty . . .

A mouse lies under Alasdair's microscope, breathing heavily, as she enters the lab shortly before noon that Friday. The animal has been scalped and has its eyes tightly closed under a layer of cream. He has peeled off the fur between its ears so that it is lying around the bloody wound like a mink. The room doesn't smell like mouse but like the dentist's because of the ointment Alasdair has used to anaesthetize the animal before implanting a miniature hard drive in its brain with tiny screws, like a goldsmith. Alasdair had been a psychologist. He switched to neurobiology to break the big questions, the WHY, down to the pragmatic ones, the HOW, he claims. When someone looks at him in amazement, he adds, The HOW is more boring than the WHY, I know, but I learnt to deal with boredom in my parents' little supermarket when I had to stock the bottom shelves after school.

What are you going to do with that hammer? Alasdair points at the tool in her hand, and she points at the mouse.

Breathing funny, isn't it?

Shit, the anaesthesia, Alasdair exclaims.

Up until then he had been calmly spreading ointment on the underside of the tiny mouse's skull, but now was nervously fiddling with a tube that led into a gas cartridge. She looks at the open wound with a mink stole and feels the need to stroke the mouse. Instead, she leans on the edge of the lab table and says, You really should get dirt allowance for that, like I used to get in the hospital on the ward with that head nurse Anna because of the shit I was allowed to scrape out of people's bums.

When was that? Alasdair puts in a new gas cartridge.

Early '80s.

Perhaps 1983? Because that's the year I was born.

Ah.

She clasps her hands behind her back. A few seconds of shock, and already a whole age has passed. She stops beside the microscope, continues to watch Alasdair, and more time passes.

Did you want something else? he finally asks without looking up.

Me?

She lets the hammer disappear behind her back.

I don't think I wanted anything. And even if I did, I forgot about it.

There is something seductive about forgetting, says Alasdair, and releases his mouse from the torture under the microscope. Now it has five days off, he carefully lifts it into a cage's straw as if putting a young rabbit back into its nest.


Later in the canteen, with Alasdair, Daniel and Tim earlier than usual, while listening to film recommendations for the weekend, she learns in passing that eight monkeys have arrived at a lab in southern Germany where an acquaintance of Daniel's works, and that the colleagues are allowed to conduct research on them.

What a mess, says Daniel.

What? asks Mike.

By the way, I know a film called *Twelve Monkeys* which is pretty wacky, Tim interjects. Bruce Willis has to travel back in time to track down a virus so that the apocalypse doesn't happen. In between, Brad Pitt jumps around like a psycho.

What a mess, Daniel repeats.

That they're monkeys, or that we didn't get them here in Berlin? she asks, while Alasdair is already changing the subject and telling them about a supposedly immortal jellyfish.

Immortality doesn't interest me at the moment, she says.

Well your hair sure looks great, Alasdair says, what are you interested in . . . ?

The small pause at the end of the question leaves room for the word *still*.

She looks at the food counter. There is fish. Instead of the girl with the angry yellow rag, an old man in a blue nylon smock is cleaning the long tables. He looks like a caretaker. Every now and then he contorts his mouth as if suffering a toothache or has difficulty swallowing. As part of her doctoral thesis, she had to study such mouth movements in the depressed and the schizophrenic. It's possible that the man has problems with his temporal lobes, but it could also be his ill-fitted dentures. The heels of his shoes are worn out. Does he still have sex? Eagerly, almost light-footedly, he wipes table after table in his crooked shoes. And then she wonders whether another old man is still having sex, namely, the one who disappeared from her life fifteen years after that 13th of March at Zoo Station, like a fist disappears when the hand opens . . .

A dozen participants have gathered at the entrance to the Trinity Cemetery early on Friday evening for the guided tour: When Time Becomes Eternity. Everyone here? a brash gentleman asks the group. She nods, for the birds over on the cemetery wall facing the road do indeed appear to be all there. Even when they finally fly off, she finds a cat is sitting on the threshold of the nursery. Where's our guide, the one in the white trousers? asks the lady with the rollator. Today she is wearing a different outfit than on Monday, a solid, ice-grey one that matches the nest of hair on her head. Surely her flat is all sterile-grey, too, garage-like, empty and so clean that it was as if she lived only to clean. The cat under the gardener's door gets up, hunches its back and runs past the market boxes with the busy lilies, boxwoods and pink porcelain flowers to the glass box for the cemetery announcements and there brushes up against one post, sometimes the other, as if the two were responsible for her sustenance. Then, with a cat's swing of the hips, she struts down the path which leads into the evening with a gentle incline. Nevertheless, a path like a magnet. Yes, time passes, and rarely in your favour, most often it runs against you, she thinks, and looks on after the cat until she hears a voice.

Which of you are here for the tour?

The woman walking hurriedly through the cemetery gate towards the waiting group is over forty, but with her round face has the air of a girl. How similar she looks to another who used to hold court in the smoking corner of the break yard back in the '70s, wearing a short, fluffy jumper that let showed off her belly button every time she moved. She was the prettiest girl in school and took whoever she wanted to the park in the evening, there where it was unkept. Later, the prettiest girl in school studied with Beuys, but ended up coming back to the city with four children in tow, no husband and her head closer to her shoulders to work as a saleswoman in the home-improvement store, gardening supplies department.

I'm standing in for my husband today, the woman says, in an aluminium-like voice, maybe because she is nervous.

Who's coming along anyway?

The woman stops in front of the small group of waiting people. She is less parchment-like than her husband was on Monday, though she is also wearing a pair of white trousers.

Everyone's coming along, the brash gentleman answers for everyone, and everyone laughs.

The friendly listener from Monday, however, is missing, she notices, while the woman lights a cigarette. No smoking, says the brash gentleman, sternly. The woman looks back without blinking.

Why? We're outdoors, aren't we?

For a moment her mouth looks as if it has been cast off. She clamps the cigarette between her lips and pulls a grey file folder out of her patchwork shoulder bag. She would like to ask the woman, Are you in a symbiotic relationship with the man you're representing here? You'll need to see a doctor soon, believe me, because the aim of such a relationship is to stop his ageing process. I know what I'm talking about. In the end, in such experiments, someone always loses out. In my case, by the way, the man in white trousers was named Viktor. Does yours have a different name?

The cat has reached the end of the incline with its hip swing and turns its raised tail towards the wide family tombs to turn off to the left, towards the narrower graves where everyone lies alone while the little lovers of half-shadows, the busy lilies, pink porcelain flowers and some freshly planted white ice begonias grow above them.

Follow me! the woman calls out. Follow me!

The group leaves. But she heads to the bus without making the turn across Schenkendorfstraße. She doesn't want to stand out in front of the lime-green closed door of No. 7 for the third time in a week.

**2.11**

Far away. Close. Past.

# SATURDAY

A group of men in suits, faces pale with domination, walk through the main hall of Tegel Airport, past the table where she is sitting alone. Today she has come here earlier than usual because the plane from Moscow on which Robert Storm will be sitting lands at 10.45 a.m. The only one on Saturday. On another bar stool, a few steps away, a woman in a blue airline uniform opens the top button of her blouse and makes a phone call. Outside, behind the panoramic window facing the street, a white VIP bus replaces a green Flix bus in the car park. She looks at the display opposite the cafe where city names, flight numbers and times spell themselves upwards from position to position, as they did last weekend and on all the weekends, in all the years and decades before. Moscow, Zurich, Istanbul. She hears the clacking of the changing positions, as if they are trying to make a statement about all the time that has passed. Her time.

An older man holding what appears to be a new folding bike stops by her table and points to the free stool.

May I?

What a question! Doesn't he see the birds that have flown together will only be driven off by a storm?

The older man must be just over seventy. She watches him as he awkwardly but lovingly pushes his folded-up bicycle under the table. What a practical companion, such a bike, only its owner lacks the nonchalance or cheerful impartiality needed for such things. Excuse me, may I? the man asks again, but he has already thrown his jacket over the back of the stool and a newspaper on the table. The skin on his elbows is dry and scabby. Like Viktor's was back then.

The older man sits down, and the birds fly off.

In front of the boutique opposite the young saleswoman, with a tired face like last Sunday, jerks her rack of twinsets until it is parallel to the shop window. Purple is available in every size. In red, only the one-piece hangs, right at the front of the rack. In the past she would never have worn red, but then there used to be yellow buckets seats here too. They're gone, there aren't any more ladybirds either, or kids roller-skating down the street between parking meters with a lollipop in their hands, or mothers wearing shoulder pads, or fathers snoring on the sofa after programming had ended for the night. Even radios with a record button no longer exist, the ones that could make tapes into tape salad. What does that prove? That in the past not everything was like it used to be either? Anyway, in the past, what a lachrymose phrase, but that's the way people are, trust me, Viktor had said once, nibbling at his elbow. Everything that's present at the time of one's birth is the natural order of things. What's invented between the ages of fifteen and thirty-five is exciting, revolutionary or advances one's career, and what comes after the age of thirty-six suddenly violates the natural order of the world.

How old was Viktor now, anyway? He too had once been thirty-six, like Robert Storm now or Johann when she met him. And all of a sudden you're old . . .

She looks at the clothes rack with the twinsets. The saleswoman has disappeared into the shop. The fact that it is still sorted the same way as last Sunday, is that a déjà vu or just a precisely stored impression, barely six days old and so banal that there is no reason to have to forget it or not to want to remember it. She saves forgetting for more important moments. For moments like the one she is about to have when she will walk in jeans and blouse past the clothes rack to the Boeing 737 from Moscow, Gate 11, through which, according to the expected arrival time, a Robert Storm must emerge after 10.45 a.m. Here I am or It's me, she will say the moment they are standing facing each other, having forgotten in the act of speaking that she has already said those words before, to one man or another. But she will say the three, or two, words as if for the first time.

Here I am.

It's me.

The moment will stand up to all past ones, and she will balance like a goddess of victory, without feeling dizzy, without any fear, on a threshold that says 10.45.

Here I am.

It's me.

I love you.

No matter what happens at 10.46 . . .

No, the older man on the stool opposite says now because a girl has stopped by the table with a note in her hand: I'm from Barbulesti, Romania and am hungry. The girl holds out her other hand, submissively, relentlessly. The saleswoman comes back out, typing into her mobile phone. Probably a message to a loved one, ending with an ILYSM—I love you so much, Raoul has explained to her. She pushes her folded hands between her thighs. What is that actually—love? A shred of eternity? Salmon singing in the street? Heartbeats in a matchbox? Or is love just a conspiratorial couple at the end of a long-forgotten film, holding hands forever as the road on which they disappear into the depths of space with their backs to the viewer narrows? Is love any different today? Have the vanishing points shifted? That it comes and goes is nothing new. Only the tempo may have changed. Love is there with a click and gone in a flash. Is that true or does she just have no idea any more?

No, the elderly man on the stool opposite repeats, rolling up his newspaper as if to swat an annoying fly. The saleswoman raises her head, having obviously heard the cut of his voice. Her tired face smiles. Others who can smile so girlishly have even been known to become German Chancellor.

No, we don't give to beggars, says the older man. Have a nice day, the girl from Barbulesti murmurs and leaves. From behind she looks like an empty skin. The man watches her go.

She's probably got lice, he says.

Probably not, she says.

Disappointed, he looks at her across the table. Then he leans towards her: Let me tell you something. If she wasn't so stupid as to say she was Roma, but said she was from Syria instead, she would get a lot more. She'd even get something from me.

How do you know she's Roma?

She had plush slippers on, didn't you see? They always wear them in Romania when they beg.

With a smile she must have borrowed from the saleswoman, she slid off the stool.

Have a nice day.

Likewise.

Now the older man doesn't look disappointed, just sullen and hard. He violently bumps his foot against his bike under the table. It falls over. But when a thing like that just falls over, it doesn't have to be a sad thing.

Gate 11. The UT Boeing 737 will be on time. A woman sits down next to her on the bench with her legs splayed. She is wearing grey overalls with neon stripes on the side seams. When the woman smiles at her, she asks: What does UT actually mean?

I don't know exactly. In any case, UTair used to be Aeroflot, also known as AeroCrap. But my husband still flies with them regularly.

The same vague delicacy resonates in her voice as it did early yesterday morning when it was still night in front of No. 7 Schenkendorfstraße.

Where does your husband fly?

Siberia.

Oh, I see, she says quietly to the pregnant woman, your husband regularly flies to Siberia, I thought so.

Why? Your husband, too?

At that moment, they both cross their legs, but only one of them suspects that there are two women waiting for Robert Storm at Gate 11 that Saturday morning. A sad three-step imposes itself:

1. the woman next to her is fat like the woman at the window last night.

2. the voice is the voice of the woman at the window.

3. so the fat woman next to her is the woman at the window last night, but in daylight she is not fat, she is pregnant.

Have you ever been to Siberia?

No, you?

Me? No, I'm afraid of flying and prefer to stay at home. You have a house?

The pregnant woman puts her hands under her belly and looks friendly.

No, I'm having a baby, but we don't have a house yet. We live in Kreuzberg, right next to the big cemetery. Why?

To me you look like an architect who designs houses with the right man to build them.

What an imagination! the pregnant woman quips. Just like my mother.

You can call me mum, like last night, she almost offered, but points to the grey overalls instead.

Nice one-piece, are they wearing them again now?

The pregnant woman says, I inherited it from my mother-in-law. When she was expecting her first child, my husband, she sewed it. It used to be the thing to do, you remember?

Yes, she replies, I'd forgotten, but now I do remember. Something she looked at a long time ago begins to speak inside her. She looks intently at the face next to her. It is as if the past is casting a light on these features, from within and from without. That's how it is with memories. *Where the wind carried him away, no one knows to say . . .*

Who are you waiting for? the pregnant woman asks.

For my husband.

She quickly looks towards the gate. Has she blushed? That hasn't happened to her in years. UT 737, she tries to sort out her thoughts, is therefore the abbreviation of the airline with which Storm will land. But UT could also be the abbreviation for a number of things. From some strange web of space and time, at that moment another pregnant woman comes back, with glorious spots on her face that a god must have sown there so that she reaps only joy. Not only was it full of freckles, that face back then, but it was also full of bright speckles of light cast by the sun through the glass roof onto her skin. She remembers: the same grey overalls now as when she first flew from Tegel in a plane. To Viktor, the terrified widower who had paid for the ticket, sent it by post and had had deposited at the counter.

She points to the woman's belly with its row of buttons stretched across it.

... and you, do you already know whether it will be a boy or a girl?

A boy, the woman says, but may I ask what your husband's name actually is? Maybe my husband and yours know each other. Maybe the two of them are often on the plane together? On Saturdays, only this one morning flight from Moscow lands here.

Johann, she answers, his name is Johann, my husband.

A nice name, the woman says.

And what's his name supposed to be?

Again she points to the pregnant woman's belly under the grey fabric.

Phone.

Sorry?

Your phone! The pregnant woman laughs. It rang. Didn't you hear it?

So, you're going to Berlin, Johann had said when she showed him the letter from the neurobiological institute that Saturday night. At that moment a light had gone on in the window of one of the nuns across the way.

It's a permanent job, Johann, she said, that means a regular income.

She pulled the small note out of her pocket that Nina had placed on the Biedermeier dresser at noon. Smoothed it out on her thigh. Over at the nuns' a second light went on.

So, you're going to Berlin, Johann repeated. Underneath the statement lay a second one: You're leaving me, Beautiful.

Do you want us to carry on as before, Johann?

He went to get another beer. Somewhere a kettle whistled so loudly from an open window into the night that gradually more and more little yellow rectangles of light flickered on in the house opposite because of the noise.

A few weeks later Johann had taken her to the train. Her furniture had already gone ahead to Berlin. Just an additional load. She didn't have much to take with her if she didn't want to take anything from Johann. She also left the bed they shared in her room and took the narrow one from the cellar that he had built for himself when he graduated from grammar school. It was the end of October. She already knew then that this bed would be her refuge, her temporary home in the future. Johann stood on the platform, she at the window. Why didn't he come with her to at least help her move in, put up the lamps and washing machine, and then stay a little longer? A week, a month, a lifetime. Was his heart even more sluggish than hers? Was that why they went their separate ways without meaning to? Had the sum of all the forces acting on them felt like zero for too long, so that a letter from Berlin weighed so much? Had they become not only precarious but lazy existences who had forgotten that a life-of-two requires the finest effort? As the train pulled away, Johann waved. She began to cry. You couldn't open an ICE window. She couldn't raise her hand and wave goodbye in the same cold air as he was in out there. Couldn't shout, Let's wave together to my intention to go to Berlin. Let's go home, hand in hand, no matter how cold it is, where the chestnuts outside our window are almost bare by now.

They talked on the phone, at first every evening, later less. Telephones do not stabilize long-distance relationships all that well, she'd already learnt that long ago. Shortly before Christmas, he came to visit her and brought the Hero-of-Labour mug with him. They went to the zoo, to see the polar bears as well. He stayed for three days, during which he did things for her in the flat but did not sleep with her. He's got someone else, she thought, and at that very moment he asked: Do you have someone else? That's when she began crying again, maybe because the thought of losing each other for someone else didn't seem so bad to her any more. They didn't even have to fall out of love any more. That's how it goes when you live apart, she'd thought, knowing that their love had been lost to them the way other people lose a stick or a hat.

In April Johann met a woman he moved to Zurich with. From there he reported by e-mail that he had been full of hatred for Switzerland from day one. In future, he wrote to Berlin, he would record his conversations with the authorities in Zurich and publish them as a docu-drama. Just try, he ranted, to re-register your car here as a foreigner, Beautiful, and you'll be arrested right away on the phone and promised a fine. Because customs is like an institution for troubled youth: If you don't follow the rules, they tell you, you'll have to pay, and then more than the few centimes for this conversation here, then we'll arrest you with your illegal German car the very next time at the border, and unfortunately your German eye test is no longer sufficient, you need an eye test from a Swiss certified optician . . . By the way, I don't smoke any more, Johann wrote, but I am driving a white Mercedes again, but with the company logo ANGST. That's a key company here. I'm a taxi driver. If you ever come here and dial seven times seven, Beautiful, I'll pick you up right away . . . That sounded hopeful and as if Johann had not been lost to her. As if he were sitting, insistent as ever, in a waiting room far away, but with her in his thoughts.

I wonder if he still drinks so much milk.

Then she had the dream: Johann was lying sideways, his knees to his stomach, on a floe broken off from the rest of the world, drifting in dark, oily water, unable to make any progress himself. But a dog was sitting with him, entirely black and more the silhouette of a dog. With its muzzle pushed towards the hem of Johann's jacket, the animal remained, no, it had become stuck in a motionless, boundless relationship to its master, and when it did lift its muzzle and looked at her . . . Oh, Johann, she wrote in an SMS the next day. He replied with something whimsical. But his cheerful tone and the fact that he didn't address her as Beautiful revealed that he would soon stop writing at all. Perhaps he had found someone more beautiful. Or the right one? Someone like Nina perhaps? Six months later he got married. Her name was Laura, and she was older than he was. An artist, he said on the phone. Then you finally got what you always wanted, she'd answered and hung up.

Well, anyway, the woman was too old to have another child with him, she told herself.

What a bleak consolation!

As she walks phone in hand through the glass door which opens with a soft smacking sound and on towards the bus stop a security notice comes on just like at any airport: Please do not leave your luggage unattended! Please advise security staff of any unattended pieces of luggage.

And any single women too, please, she hears a voice at the other end of the line say. Are you there at Tegel? Theres Grau asks. You doing OK?

Why?

I just had a feeling.

Oh, spirit-seer of mine, can you hear the grass whispering and the fleas coughing?

Audibly walking through her little end rowhouse Theres says, we don't have any fleas here. A drawer is pulled open. Cutlery rattles. Perhaps she has already brewed coffee in the tradition of her Slavic grandmother, stirred powder, sugar and hot water into one another and drunk the brew, only to read the future—or at least a colleague's Saturday state of mind—from the sentence on the bottom of the cup without being asked. A toaster clicks. Surely her boyfriend is waiting for Theres to finally stop talking to the world outside. Because it's colder underneath the table at breakfast without her.

Theres says, Do you know what I just read? Women over thirty-five are often haunted by five minutes of anxiety, almost daily at night. Being alone is bad for your health.

I am not thirty-five.

She turns to the bench in front of Gate 11, and doesn't really listen to Theres continue.

The pregnant woman is still sitting there, alone and leaning a little to one side. She leans on the neighbouring seat with one hand, as if to keep it free.

What are you actually calling about? she interrupts Theres as she takes a few steps outside along the access road. What a day. It's a pity this sunlight at the end of August can't be scooped up with a bucket.

A man has broken away from a group of men standing around a taxi and is coming towards her. He is rolling a cigarette in one hand while silently flicking the other in the air to ask for a light. She pulls the found object from Thursday's movie night out of her jacket pocket. As the Zippo opens with a metallic clack, Theres clears her throat.

You smoke? Did I hear that right?

Yes, she lies back.

And smoking helps?

The man bends over the flame with his cigarette.

What helps, she thinks, is the way he's squinting just now, looking like someone who can probably love as devotedly as he smokes and plays football.

It'll pass, Theres Grau says rather slowly against her ear. At the same pace, the man saunters back to his taxi colleagues, smoking, and nods to her again once he's there. Surely he too is a melancholy thirty-six.

It'll pass, Theres repeats.

What will pass?

I've already been through it, Theres replies, but I was never at the mercy of it all like you. I mean, I have a boyfriend, we want a family. That helps.

Lucky you, she lies again. I'm going to call it a day. She simply pushes Theres away.

By the time she turns around to Gate 11 the pregnant woman has disappeared. She goes back to the bench, sits down and stays there until UTair Flight 737 has also disappeared from the display. A single traveller comes out of the exit with a wheeled suitcase around which he has wrapped a ribbon with a carabiner that looks like an elastic tow rope. But it is not Robert Storm. Surely Storm has disappeared around the corner there with cheerful impartiality, hooked into his wife waddling like a duck beside him.

Far away, close, past.

She did not even walk up to him briefly, casually brush his arm and say: There was dust on your jacket. I like your suit, promise me never you'll never wear white trousers because I like your suit, I like it a lot. Are the pockets still sewn shut?

She looks down the row of numbered exits. Time to go.

Two policemen are checking a young man at Gate 9, who is running a hand through his hair, hair like raven feathers and skin that is brown even without the sun. He pulls the sleeves of a thin blue rain jacket up over his fingers and shakes his head. He looks cold. She walks past him, then on through the main hall . . .

**21.11**

Tegel Airport. I make my way through the main hall towards the bus stop.

Outside. No storm, just weather.

## Acknowledgements

I would like to thank Andreas Draguhn, Susanne Feldmann, Thomas Fuchs, Mathias Greffrath, Lilo Gegic, Hannah Monyer, Dag Moskopp, Gabriele Thielker, Barbara Wild, Laura Winkels as well as Wolfgang Herrndorf on behalf of all those authors whose texts accompanied the work on this novel.

Judith Kuckart
*January 2019*

*Translator's Notes*

**PAGE 5** | Tegel Airport: was located in the western half of Berlin. Commercial services began in 1960 and ended in 2020.

**PAGE 10** | 'Only this one thing was plain . . . never seen again': 'The Story of Flying Robert' is an episode in Heinrich Hoffmann's 1845 children's book, *Der Struwwelpeter*, published in English in 1848 as *Shockheaded Peter*, and from where the name Robert Storm is derived.

**PAGE 18** | 'hooked on *The Story of Christiane F.*': refers to *Wir Kinder vom Bahnhof Zoo* (translated into English by Christina Cartwright as *Zoo Station: The Story of Christiane F.*), a 1979 book chronicling the real-life story of a teenage girl caught up in the world of heroin dependency and prostitution set in Bahnhof Zoo, the main train station in West Berlin, between 1975 and 1978. The book, and the 1981 film of the same name, caused a sensation. An updated TV-version appeared in early 2021.

**PAGES 59–60** | 'For, nearing death . . . then break down ourselves': from Rainer Maria Rilke's 'Eighth Duino Elegy' in *The Selected Poetry of Rainer Maria Rilke* (Stephen Mitchell ed. and trans.) (New York: Random House, 1980).

PAGE **84** | 'Yeah, a *meister* from Germany': is a reference to Paul Celan's poem 'Death Fugue'.

PAGE **162** | 'A lift to the scaffold': refers to Louis Malle's 1958 film *Ascenseur Pour L'Echafaud*, starring Jeanne Moreau and Maurice Ronet—the soundtrack by Miles Davis is legendary.

PAGE **168** | 'Whoever laughs at fairy tales, was never in distress': from Alexander Kluge's film *Die Patriotin*.

PAGE **176** | 'It is nonsense . . . says love': lines from the poem 'Was es ist' (What it is) by Erich Fried.